ANGEL EYES

#2

DEATH'S ANGEL

Also by Robert J. Randisi

ANGEL EYES

#2

DEATH'S ANGEL

Robert J. Randisi

SPEAKING VOLUMES, LLC

NAPLES, FLORIDA

2012

ANGEL EYES

#2 DEATH'S ANGEL

ISBN 978-1-61232-584-2

To my Angel Eyes, Anna, and our little angel, Christopher.

#2

ANGEL EYES

DEATH'S ANGEL

CHAPTER ONE

ANGEL EYES could see that the young rider wouldn't be able to stay ahead of her two pursuers much longer. Their larger and more powerful horses were cutting into the distance between them and the girl with every stride.

Liz watched the action from her vantage point on a grassy knoll. She didn't know any of the facts, but she couldn't believe that the girl — who appeared from this distance to be in her late teens — could have done anything to warrant two burly men chasing her with such determination.

Liz really had no choice but to intercede on the girl's behalf.

With the heels of her boots Liz spurred Blossom into a run, calculating the angle she'd have to take to come between the girl and her pursuers. The big bay mare loved to run and was very fast. It was no problem for Liz and Blossom to intercept the two men and force them to a halt.

"What the hell — !" one of the men shouted, reining his horse in violently to keep from running into Liz. His friend was forced to rein in also to avoid running up the first man's back. Both men were thickly built and in their mid-thirties, with faces not even a mother would love.

"Hold up!" Liz called.

"Get out of our way, lady," the first man demanded.

"Not until I get some answers."

"Answers? What kind of answers?"

"Why are you chasing that young girl?"

"Seems to me that ain't none of your business," the first man said. "And if you don't move out of my way, I'm gonna ride right over you."

"I'd like to see you try it."

The first man had a scar running diagonally across his face from his left temple to the right side of his chin. When his face turned red with anger, as it did now, the scar showed up as a starkly white line.

Liz got the distinct impression that the man was upset.

"Lady," he said tightly, "I ain't gonna tell you again. Move!"

"Not until you answer my question," Liz said. She appeared totally relaxed.

"I told you — " the man said, and Liz watched as his hand moved toward his gun.

"I wouldn't do that," she said.

"Why not?" he demanded.

"Because I'd have to kill you."

"You'd what — ?" he began, but the second man moved his horse up next to the first and whispered something Liz couldn't hear. The first man looked at Liz sharply, and only then did she realize that her orange bandana, which she usually kept rolled up and tucked inside her collar, had come loose and fallen out from inside her shirt.

"All right, lady," the first man said. "You helped her get away from us, and you're gonna be sorry for it, but I guess today ain't the day."

"As far as you're concerned," she replied, "never is closer than you'll ever get to making me sorry."

"We'll see," he said, and pulled on the reins to turn his horse.

"Hold it," Liz said.

"Now what?"

Liz turned her head to look behind her and saw that the girl had reined in her horse and was watching from a safe distance. The men could still circle around and take after her again — if Liz left them on horseback.

"I think I'd like you boys to step down from your horses."

"What's that?" said the man with the scar.

"Down," she said. "Now."

"Now, that's going too — " the man started, but broke off when his friend again leaned over to whisper something. Then Scarface shook his companion off impatiently and snapped, "I don't care who she is!"

"Mister," Liz said in her most school-marmish tone, "why don't we make this easier on all of us and just do as we're told."

The man glared at her. "You know, I'd like to try you right here and now."

"Be my guest."

They exchanged looks for a few seconds and then the man said, "My friend here doesn't want me to, so you lucked out."

"Sure," she said. "Now the two of you just step down and take off your boots."

At this, the man with the scar paused in the act of dismounting. His head snapped up. "Jesus Christ!" he protested.

"Tracy, please!" the second man said. It was the first time he'd spoken aloud. "I want to live to get back to town."

At that the first man complied, grumbling as he sat on the ground to remove his boots.

"Put them in your saddlebags."

They obeyed.

Liz moved forward to collect the reins of the two horses. "How far to town?" she inquired.

"Couple of miles that way," the second man said, pointing south.

"Okay," she said. "I'm going to tie your horses off a couple of miles to the north. It's your choice which way you walk."

"I ain't going back to town without my horse and boots," Scarface said.

"That's fine," she said. "You should feel lucky I'm leaving you your guns — which, by the way, neither of you should touch until I'm well out of range."

"Everything went your way this time, lady," Scarface said. "But there'll be a next time."

"That's something for you to look forward to," Liz said. "I've got other plans."

Liz rode on to where the young girl was now waiting — still a bit skittish from the looks of her. When she reached the girl Liz saw that she was about seventeen and pretty as a chestnut filly.

"How did you do that?" the girl asked.

"What?"

"That," the girl said, pointing. "How did you get them to give you their horses and their boots?"

"I asked them."

"You couldn't have just — "

"What's your name?"

"Angie," the girl said. "Angie Carter."

"Why were they chasing you, Angie?"

"Come on home with me," Angie said. "Pa's gonna want to meet you anyway after what you done. We'll tell you the whole thing."

Liz thought it over for a moment and then said, "All right. We'll leave their horses a couple of miles from here and then I'll take you home."

"That's great," Angie said eagerly, then added, "My pa's gonna like you."

Andrew Carter was worried.

Angie was headstrong, like her mother had been, and she was lovely — probably even more lovely than her mother, if that was possible. He had told her constantly not to go riding by herself, yet she had taken off that morning to God only knew where. Here it was afternoon and she wasn't back yet.

That was cause enough to worry, even without the problems they'd been having of late.

Carter had just walked out onto his porch for what seemed the hundredth time when he spotted the dust cloud. As the cloud drew closer, he waited with bated breath until he could see the rider — no, riders. One was certainly Angie; the other he didn't know. She was blonde and she sat her bay mare confidently.

When the two women reached the house, Carter stepped down off the porch and took hold of the reins of Angie's horse, a chestnut mare she called Brandy.

"I ought to tan your hide, young lady," he said as she dropped to the ground. The other woman dismounted more gracefully. Close up he could see that she was not so very much older than Angie.

"But you won't," Angie said, throwing her arms around her father's neck and kissing him on the cheek.

He gave her a stern look that dissolved into a smile; then he hugged her.

"I was worried."

"You had cause," the blonde woman said, stepping forward.

"Why?" He looked at Angie. "What happened?"

"Oh, Pa," Angie said, "You won't believe what Liz just did for me."

"Liz?"

"Liz Archer," the woman said, introducing herself.

"I'm Andrew Carter, Miss Archer," he replied. "And if you've helped my daughter I'm very grateful."

"Let's go inside, Pa," Angie said, pulling on his arm. "I've got to tell you. Oh, I invited Liz to eat with us. Is that all right?"

Andrew Carter studied the blonde young woman for a few moments before answering. She looked to be in her early twenties, a very lovely and self-possessed young woman with incredible eyes.

"I don't see why not," he said. "Come on inside."

Liz smiled at him. "I'd better just take care of the horses first."

"I can have someone — "

"No, I'd like to," she said, taking up the reins of both horses. "I'll be right with you."

"All right," said Carter. He put his arm absently around Angie as they walked inside, the pretty blonde stranger weighing on his mind.

CHAPTER TWO

LIZ WAS TROUBLED as she took care of the horses in the livery. Although Angie's father had to be at least in his early forties, he seemed to Liz to be a vibrant, striking-looking man and, to her dismay, she found herself instantly attracted to him. It didn't bother her that he was older than she was by twenty years, or so. But it did bother her that she felt an instant attraction to the man. She had not had much luck with men in the past and had frankly been staying away from them.

After she had groomed and fed the two horses, she turned to leave and found herself facing a man who was watching her curiously. He was short, but built very wide and low to the ground. She had the feeling that it would need at least two men to take him off his feet.

''New hand?'' he asked. His voice was raspy, as if he had been hit in the throat a lot.

"No," she said. "I'm a . . . a guest."

The man had dark, brooding eyes and a firm jaw and gave off an aura of menace. He had large, blunt-fingered hands and wore an old Walker Colt on his hip. The gun reminded her of her father's, the one she'd used to kill her first man.

"I'll walk you to the house," the man said then, "just to make sure."

In spite of his menacing appearance she was impressed by his controlled manner. He had found a stranger in the livery but, as she had obviously been putting something in and not taking something out, he had approached her quietly and calmly.

"My name is Liz Archer," she said as they walked back to the house together.

"I'm Ridge."

"You work here," Liz said, making it a statement rather than a question. She knew he worked there, but she didn't know in what capacity.

As they approached the house he said, "Yeah. I'm the foreman."

She stepped up onto the wooden porch and said, looking down at him, "Then you knew I wasn't a new hand."

"I wanted to see if you'd lie."

"And I didn't."

"No, you didn't."

At that point Andrew Carter came out and stared at both of them.

"Is there a problem, Ridge?"

"No problem, Mr. Carter. Saw a stranger in the barn and asked her some questions, is all."

Carter looked at Liz for confirmation and she nodded and said, "We've been getting acquainted."

"I see," he said. He looked back at his foreman. "Miss Archer is a guest, Ridge . . . and a friend," he said. "She has the run of the place."

"Fine," Ridge replied. He touched the front of his battered gray hat to Liz and then turned and left.

"Come in. I've made some coffee."

"Sounds good."

As they entered Carter said, "You *will* stay for dinner?"

"I don't want to be a — "

"Nonsense," he said, placing his hand against the small of her back. "You're staying."

"All right."

She felt his hand tremble slightly against her back, and she knew that the attraction she had been feeling was not one-sided.

Dinner was prepared by Angie, who turned out to be a very good cook.

"I cook and clean real good," she said at one point. "But I can ride and rope much better."

"That's the truth," Andrew Carter said. "Angie got it into her mind at an early age that I wanted a son, and she's been practically a son and a daughter ever since."

Angie smiled fondly at her father and then looked at Liz. "Why do you think he named me Angie?" she said.

"Ang — "

"Let's not argue about it, Pa," Angie said. "Not in front of our guest."

Andrew Carter looked over at Liz, who said, "There is something else I'd like to talk about, if we can."

"What's that?"

"Why those two men were chasing Angie."

Carter looked at Angie and the two exchanged a long,

searching glance during which Liz could have sworn they were communicating. Liz understood that. It had been that way between her and her brother at times, as if they could almost read each other's minds.

"That's not something you should get involved with, Liz," Andrew Carter finally said.

"The way I see it I'm already involved," Liz replied. "Those two men we saw today are not likely to forget me."

"She's got a point, Pa."

Carter looked at his daughter again, then nodded and said, "All right. I guess you do deserve an explanation."

"Legal landgrabbing?" Liz asked.

"That's what I call it," Carter said. "You see, James Morris has bought up as many mortgages as he can in the area, knowing that a lot of ranchers are having trouble making their payments. It's not something new."

"And when they can't pay he takes over?"

"Right."

"And if they can pay?"

"If he gets tired of waiting," Angie spoke up, "he sends some of his men in to harass them."

"Like with you today?"

"This is the first time they've come after me," the girl said. "But they've harassed Pa before."

Liz looked at Andrew Carter, who said, "Little things like running off some of our beef, salting small water holes, breaking fences. They're just trying to get me and some of the others who have been able to scrape the mortgage money together to leave."

"How long can you keep scraping?"

"Not much longer, I'm afraid," he said, shaking his head. Angie reached across the table to cover one of her father's hands with hers. "If they escalate their harassment, I don't think I'll be able to make the next one. Not if they force any added expenses on us."

"I see," Liz said, and then added, "Has there been any violence up to now?"

"Nothing fatal," Carter said. "They've picked fights with some hands in town — sent them back beaten up and unable to work for a few days."

"How many hands do you have besides Ridge?"

"Not too many, but we're a small spread. I've got five or six men working for me."

"Have they tried buying any of them off?"

"Not that we know of, but I guess that's to be expected somewhere along the way. If I lose a hand or two that'll slow me down."

"You run cows?"

He nodded and said, "Yes. But mainly horses."

"Pa's a great horseman."

"We sell to the army, and to some private concerns. The beef we run is just to supplement that."

Liz nodded and thought to herself that James Morris sounded like just another bully.

"It's getting late," she said. "I'd better be heading for town to find a room — "

"Oh, no," Angie said. "You're staying here with us. Isn't she, Pa?"

"If she likes," Carter said, looking at Liz. "We have room."

"I don't want to put you out — "

"You're not!" Angie said. "Please. If you stay you and I can talk longer. There aren't many girls around here close to my age. I know you're older, but you ain't that much older . . . are you?"

Liz laughed and said, "No, I'm not that much older."

"Then it's settled?" Angie said. "You'll stay?"

"I'll stay," Liz said, and then after a moment added, "The night."

James Morris glared at the two sweaty, bedraggled men standing before him in his office; both of them were staring at the floor.

"A woman," Morris said. "You had your horses taken away from you by a woman."

The man with the scar, Jack Tracy, said, "At least we told you the truth, boss."

"This time maybe you should have lied."

"Boss — " began the other man, Lon Clarke.

"Oh, shut up, both of you. I don't know if I can keep men on my payroll who can't handle a woman."

"She wasn't just any woman, boss," Lon said quickly.

"That's what he told me out there, boss," Tracy said. "And he still ain't told me just *who* she is."

"All right, I'll take the bait," Morris said. "Who is she?"

"A blonde woman" Lon said, "with an orange bandana, wearing a gun."

"Wait a minute," Morris said, holding up one well-manicured hand. "That rings a bell. What's her name?"

"See," Lon said, as much to Tracy as to his boss. "It sounded familiar to me, too, but I can't think of her name."

"So what?"

"She's killed men in gunfights — "

"All right, you two, that's enough," Morris said, cutting them off and dismissing them. "Get out of here, get cleaned up and have something to eat. Be ready to work in the morning."

"Yessir," Tracy said. "Come on, Lon."

"My achin' feet — " Lon was saying as the two men shuffled out of Morris's office.

"Shut up!" Tracy snapped.

Paragon, Wyoming, was like any other progressive town in the west. It was growing by leaps and bounds, and when that happened there was usually somebody trying to keep one step ahead of it.

James T. Morris was a self-made man. Everything he had he had gotten by taking it, using whatever means necessary. In his late thirties now, he was a handsome man, but one who worried about growing old. His hair was neatly trimmed and his nails were manicured — he had them done twice a week to keep them that way. He dressed impeccably, usually wearing three-piece suits in various shades of brown. Black, he maintained, was for gamblers, and he never gambled. That would mean leaving things to chance, and he never did that.

He disliked chance, and that was why he doubted that the appearance of this woman — the blonde with the orange bandana whose name he couldn't remember any more than Lon could — was purely by chance.

If his memory served him correctly, she *had* killed men in a gunfight or two. Was she for hire? Had Carter decided to hire himself a gun?

If that were indeed the case, then perhaps it was time for James T. Morris to hire one of his own, as well.

And he knew just the man.

CHAPTER THREE

LIZ WOKE TO THE wonderful aroma of cooking eggs and bacon and brewing coffee.

"That smells wonderful," she said, entering the kitchen and finding Angie at the stove.

"Sit down. It's almost ready," Angie said cheerfully. "How did you sleep?"

"Considering my guilt for taking your bed, I slept just fine."

"Oh, I slept just fine out here," Angie said, indicating the blanket and bedroll rolled up in a corner of the room.

"Is your father up?"

"Up and out. He'll be back for breakfast, though. I told him he had to eat with our guest."

"You shouldn't have done that, Angie," Liz said. "Your father has a lot of work to do."

"He's got to eat," the younger girl argued. "So he might as well eat with you."

Angie brought Liz a cup of coffee to start with.

"It was great talking to you last night, Liz," she said. "It's been such a long time since I've had someone to talk to."

"You mean you don't have any boyfriends?"

"In this town?" She made a disgusted sound. "Around here they're either boys or older men — not that there's anything wrong with older men. Don't you agree?"

Liz had a pretty good idea where that question was leading, but was saved from answering by Andrew Carter's arrival.

"Good morning."

"Morning," Liz greeted him.

"That smells wonderful, honey," he said, kissing his daughter's forehead.

"Sit down. I was just about to serve Liz."

Angie proceeded to set out two plates of bacon, eggs and biscuits.

"Aren't you eating?" Liz asked.

"I've eaten," Angie said. "I've got to ride into town this morning and do some shopping."

"Alone?" Carter asked. "Damn it, I've warned you about that, Angie. Didn't you learn anything yesterday — ?"

"Wait, I'll go with you — " Liz started to say, standing up.

"Will you both relax?" Angie said, putting one hand on a shoulder of each. "I'm not going alone; Ridge is going with me. I need him to pack the wagon."

Both Carter and Liz sat back down in their chairs, feeling rather sheepish.

"All right, I'm sorry," Carter said to his daughter. "But remember not to spend too much."

"Don't worry, Pa," Angie said. "You know I'm very good with money."

"That's true," Carter agreed, looking at Liz.

"All right, you two, start eating," Angie said. "You can talk to each other. I'll be back a little later. Liz, you'll be here, won't you?"

"I'll wait for you, Angie."

"Good."

Angie picked up her hat and said, "See you later. Get acquainted while I'm gone."

After Angie flew out of the door Andrew Carter looked at Liz and said, "I'm sorry about that. For the last few years Angie has been something of a would-be matchmaker. I hope you're not embarrassed."

"I'm not," Liz said. "Are you?"

"Actually," Carter said, staring across the table into Liz's incredible blue eyes, "I'm not."

"Then let's eat."

Angie took the buckboard into town while Ridge rode along behind her. When they reached town she pulled to a stop in front of the General Store, and Ridge rode up alongside.

"I'm gonna have a drink in the saloon," he said. "I'll be back in time to load up."

"No hurry, Ridge."

"We gotta get back," was all he said, and then turned his horse toward the saloon without dismounting to help Angie down.

Two men sauntering along across the street suddenly stopped to watch Angie Carter enter the General Store.

"Hey, Lon," Jack Tracy said, grabbing his partner's arm.

"What?"

"That Carter kid just went into the General Store."

Lon Clarke grinned and said, "She ain't no kid, Tracy. If the boss hadn't said hands off I could — "

"Forget that," Tracy said, impatiently. "We was supposed to do a job yesterday and we didn't do it."

"Thanks to that blonde."

"Right. But maybe we can get it done today."

"Why not?" Lon said. "She's here, ain't she?"

"Let's go," Tracy said, and both men started across the street.

Angie Carter's back was to the door as Tracy and Lon entered the store. Engrossed in discussing the price of flour with Mr. Jennings, who ran the store, she was unaware of the presence of the two men until the look on the store-keeper's face changed.

"What's wrong?" she asked.

What was wrong was that Jennings had seen these two men start trouble before, and was afraid that they were about to do so again.

"What do you want?" he demanded, but Jack Tracy brushed by Angie to stand in front of her while Lon grabbed her from behind.

"Take a walk, Jennings," Tracy said, pushing the elderly storekeeper away without even looking at him.

"This is my store — " Jennings said, putting up token resistance, but when Tracy, turning around, made eye contact with the smaller man, the storekeeper edged away until he disappeared into the back room.

"What do you jaspers want?" Angie demanded.

"We had some business to take care of yesterday, little lady," Jack Tracy said, placing a finger beneath her chin. Angie tossed her head in an effort to break the contact, accidentally striking Lon Clarke's nose with painful force and causing his eyes to water.

"Damn!" Lon shouted. He pushed Angie away from him with enough force to knock her to the floor and covered his face with his hands. When he looked at his hands and saw blood on them, he became even angrier.

"Take it easy, Lon," Tracy said, stepping between his partner and the fallen young woman.

"I'm gonna fix her — "

"Wait!" Tracy said, placing both hands against the other man's chest. He looked at Angie over his shoulder and said, "We got interrupted yesterday, sweetheart, so now we're gonna finish what we started."

"You didn't even get started yesterday," Angie sneered. "And if you touch me Liz will fill you full of lead."

"Liz?"

"Liz Archer," Angie said. "The lady who took your horses and guns from you. She's working for me and my pa."

"Liz Archer," Lon said, wiping blood from his face. "Now I know who she is!"

"Who?" Tracy asked.

"The blonde!" Lon Clarke said. "Damn. I knew that orange bandana meant something."

"Well, who is she, damn it?" Tracy said.

"Yes, who?" Angie asked, confused. She thought Liz Archer was just Liz Archer. What were these two men talking about?

"Angel Eyes," Lon said. "That's what they call her. Angel Eyes."

"I've heard that name — " Tracy began.

"I haven't," Angie said from the floor.

Hearing her speak reminded the two men why they were there.

"Well, Angel Eyes or not," Tracy said, "we got to finish what we was interrupted in the middle of yesterday."

"Yeah, but — "

"Your nose is still bleeding, Lon."

"Damn!" the man cried, putting one hand to his nose again.

"All right," Tracy said, stepping away from his partner, who began immediately to advance on Angie.

"I'm afraid you boys are gonna be interrupted again," a man's voice said from the door.

The two men and the girl on the floor all turned their heads to see Ridge filling the doorway with his bulk.

"This ain't your affair, Ridge," Tracy said.

"Yes, it is," Ridge said. "You boys better think careful about what you're gonna do. Do you want her enough to go through me first?"

"She made my nose bleed!" Lon complained.

"You make my heart bleed," Ridge said sarcastically, pinning the man with his brooding stare.

Ridge moved forward out of the doorway and across the room. Tracy took a few steps sideways to avoid him. Ridge, he knew, was tremendously strong. Lon, slower to remember that strength, received a vicious backhand that literally knocked him off his feet and split both of his lips.

"Now you've got something to complain about," Ridge said. He turned to Tracy, who backed slowly away. "Take Lon out of here, Tracy," Ridge said. "And tell your boss to leave Angie Carter be. If he wants to fight her father, that's something else, but if he goes after this girl he's gonna have to get by me first."

"Sure, Ridge, sure," Tracy said, grabbing his partner's arm and pulling him to his feet.

"What — ?"

"Come on, Lon, come on," Tracy said, urging the groggy man toward the door.

Ridge turned, reached down, took both of Angie's hands and helped her to her feet.

"Are you all right?" he asked. The concern in his eyes was new to her; she was puzzled by it. Ridge's eyes had always been so cold before. Surprised, she stared at him for a moment, her eyes wide.

"Yes, yes, I'm fine," she said at last, brushing off the seat of her pants. "I'm just getting tired of having to be rescued from those two yahoos."

"They won't be bothering you any more," the foreman said confidently.

Angie was a tall girl and Ridge was a couple of inches shorter than she was. Still, she had seen what he'd just done to the two men — scaring them out of their wits — and she could feel the power in his work-roughened hands.

Easing her hands out of his she said, "Yes, but my pa — "

"Your pa's a man," Ridge said. "He can take care of himself. Now let's get this wagon loaded and get back to the ranch."

CHAPTER FOUR

WHEN LIZ AND ANDREW CARTER finished breakfast, Liz insisted on washing the dishes.

"Nonsense," Carter said, rising from the table. For a moment she thought he was going to offer to help, but instead he added, "Angie can take care of them when she gets home."

"Is that a fact?"

She saw him stop short, and suspected it was more because of her tone than her words.

"Did I say something wrong?"

"Would it hurt you to help her a little with the housework?"

"Housework?" he said. "I've got some horses out there that need tending to."

"And I'll bet she could take care of them almost as well as you can," Liz cut in. "Could you take care of the dishes as well as she could?"

She knew that her tone held a challenge. Carter paused, considering her words.

"All right," he said at last, rolling up his sleeves. "Let's get at those dishes and you can tell me."

Smiling angelically Liz followed him to the sink.

"I didn't expect Ridge to be a problem." James Morris frowned. "He usually keeps to himself."

"Well, not this time," Jack Tracy said. "You should have seen the way he rushed to help that Carter brat."

"Look what he did to me!" Lon Clarke said, through mashed lips and broken teeth.

"Shut up," Morris said. "You look better that way."

Tracy and Lon had gone directly to James Morris's office from the General Store to tell him what had happened. Tracy had done all the talking because Lon was holding a handkerchief to his nose and mouth, trying to stem the red tide that poured forth from both apertures.

"Ridge could be a big problem," Morris went on. "Nobody in town can predict what he'll do."

"And then there's the girl," Tracy said.

"What girl?"

"The one who butted in yesterday. Her name's Liz Archer, but they call her — "

"Angel Eyes," Morris said, with a sudden flash of recognition.

"Yeah," Tracy said, looking hurt at not having been able to spring a surprise on his boss.

"Damn," Morris, said, running his right thumb back and forth over his lower lip.

"On top of that," Tracy continued, hoping to tell his boss at least one thing he didn't know, "the Carter girl says that the lady gunfighter is working for her and her pa."

"Then I was right," Morris said.

"You were?" Tracy asked glumly. "About what, boss?"

"About them hiring a gun," Morris said, rubbing his hands together. "Do you know what that means?"

"No, what?"

"Of course not; you're too stupid to figure it out," Morris said. "It means we can stop tip-toeing around this thing. Andrew Carter has been a thorn in my side since I started buying up land through the bank. His ranch is right in the center of *my* land."

"So?"

"So now I can stop trying to ease it out from under him," Morris said happily, "and just take it. I can take it because he made the first wrong move. He brought in the first hired gun."

"And now you're gonna bring in one?"

"Right."

"Who?"

"I've already sent him a telegram," Morris said, "and he's on his way."

"Who?"

"I don't care who Carter has; whether it's Angel Eyes or . . . Tate Gilmore."

"Gilmore," Tracy said, shuddering at the sound of the famed gunman's name. "So who'd you get, boss?"

"Soon," James Morris said, "very soon this Angel Eyes won't be facing you two idiots; she'll be facing a gun who's already killed more men than she'll ever lay with — Griff Taylor!"

Griff Taylor put down the telegram again on the table by the bed and reached eagerly for the girl next to him.

"Why do you keep reading that telegram?" she asked as he palmed her full, firm breasts, popping the stiff nipples with his thumbs. The skin of his hands was rough and her breasts were feather soft to the touch.

"It's a job offer, sweetheart," he said, squeezing her breasts so hard that she closed her eyes, bit her bottom lip and moaned.

"Ooh, Griff —"

Her name was Melanie Sykes and she was a tall, full-bodied brunette who Griffin Taylor visited every time he was in Cold Springs, Montana. No whore, she worked as a waitress in the Cold Spring Cafe and she had several men who visited her from time to time when they were in the county.

Griff was her favorite.

"How did whoever sent the telegram know they'd find you here?"

"My business depends on certain people knowing where I am," Taylor said. He leaned over and licked the nipple of her right breast and then the nipple of her left. He hadn't allowed her to bathe after he'd picked her up at work, he enjoyed the taste of the dried perspiration on her breasts.

"Are you going to take the job?" she asked, although she had no idea how Griffin Taylor made his living. Physically they could not have gotten closer during the year they had known each other, but in other ways Taylor never allowed her to get close — at all!

He shrugged at her question and said, "There's a lot of money involved; but I'd have to leave here tomorrow."

"You just got here yesterday," she complained.

"I know," he said, kissing her. For a big, rough-looking man, she thought, he had the gentlest kiss . . .

"If you take the job, what will happen?" she asked, moving closer to him.

"I'll have enough money to maybe take some time off," he answered.

"And spend it here?" she asked dreamily as he nuzzled the smooth, fragrant flesh of her long neck.

"Maybe."

"Well," she said, wrapping her arms around him and pressing her full breasts against his chest. She reached between them and took hold of his rigid cock, stroking it up and down with her hand until she could feel him pulsating. "At least we have today."

That was when Griff Taylor decided to leave the next morning for Paragon, Wyoming.

CHAPTER FIVE

ANGIE'S FATHER was out chasing down strays when Angie and Ridge returned to the house. Liz watched from the window as the girl and the man exchanged a few words. Then Ridge took his horse and Angie's to the livery.

"Where's Pa?" Angie asked as she entered.

"Working."

"I'll get the breakfast dishes," she said, heading for the sink.

"They're done."

"You did them?"

"Me and your pa."

Angie stared at Liz and then said, "*My* pa did the dishes?"

"He did," Liz said. "And he did a good job, too."

Angie went over to look at them and when she found that they were quite clean and free from grease she turned and said, "You did 'em."

"Well," Liz said, grinning, "he dried them."

"Liz, can I ask you something?"

"Sure, Angie."

Angie sat down at the table and Liz sat across from her.

"Can you explain men to me?"

Liz laughed and said, "I don't think anyone could explain men."

"Well, you've had experience with men, haven't you?" Angie asked.

"Some."

"Then you can help me."

"I can try, Angie," Liz said, reaching across and touching the girl's hand. "What happened?"

Angie explained to Liz what had happened in the General Store, and how Ridge had helped her.

"The same two men?"

"Yeah, but that's not what's bothering me."

"It's bothering me," Liz said. "And it'll bother your pa, too."

"Ridge bothers me."

"Ridge? You're lucky he was there."

"I know that, but afterward he acted . . . funny."

"What do you mean, funny?"

"I mean . . . strange. He had a strange look in his eyes."

"What kind of look?"

"You've seen his eyes."

"Yeah."

"What do they look like to you?"

After a moment's thought Liz came up with the only word that seemed to fit.

"Cold."

"That's the way they always looked to me too," Angie said. "Until today."

"How'd they look today?"

Angie frowned and then said, "Warm. When he helped me up they looked warm, and concerned."

Liz frowned. Ridge was in his thirties and he wasn't a good-looking man. Could it be that the foreman had a soft spot for the boss's daughter?

"Maybe he *was* concerned, Angie. After all, you're the boss's daughter."

Angie frowned, thought it over and said, "Well, maybe that's it."

"What do you think of Ridge, Angie?"

"Ridge? He's Pa's foreman; has been for a long time. I've known him since I was ten." She shrugged and repeated, "He's Pa's foreman."

Liz studied Angie's face and saw that the young woman really felt just that way about the man. He was just her father's foreman.

She felt sorry for Ridge if he felt any different about the boss's daughter.

"Hey, Liz, are you gonna stay a while?" Angie asked, changing the subject.

"I don't think so, Angie," Liz said. "Not here, anyway. I think I'll go into town."

"What for?"

"I've never seen Paragon before," Liz said, although that wasn't her real reason.

"When are you gonna leave?"

"Now," Liz said, standing up. "I was just waiting for you to get back."

"What'll I tell Pa?"

"I've already told your pa, Angie," Liz said, picking up her hat and saddlebags. "He knows I'm going."

"Do you like Pa?"

Liz looked at Angie Carter and said, "I like you both, Angie."

"Yeah, but — "

"I'll see you in Paragon, Angie," Liz said, opening the door. "I'll see you both in Paragon."

Liz wondered what Angie would have said if she knew what had happened between her and her father while she was in town.

It had happened while they were finishing up the dishes, while they were just making conversation. Liz was willing to bet that it was the furthest thing from either of their minds — consciously, that is. Although there *had* been that initial attraction they'd both felt upon first meeting.

Carter had dried the last dish and set it aside when he turned to Liz and said, "Angie likes you, you know. She's very impressed with you."

"I like her, too," Liz said, smiling. And then she heard herself asking, without shame, "What about you?"

"What about me?"

"Do *you* like me?" she asked, looking him straight in the eye.

Carter matched her gaze and said, "Yes, I like you, Liz. I like you very much."

"Well," Liz said, feeling rather awkward now, "that's good."

She started to turn away then, but when he took hold of her arm and pulled her to him, she went willingly. She was surprised how willingly she went, first into his arms, and then to his bed . . .

She was very impressed with his physique. For a man who was past forty he had a hard, well-conditioned body. Rubbing her breasts against his chest she could feel his hair rough against her sensitive, swollen nipples. She enjoyed the strength in his arms as he wrapped them around her. His mouth was firm and strong when he kissed her and she eagerly sought out his tongue with hers . . .

When he moved atop her and entered her he did so in one quick lunge, spearing her to the core. She caught her breath, closed her eyes and wrapped her arms and legs around him, matching his tempo perfectly. It had been a long time for her, a long time since that first time with Tate Gilmore—her very first time—and the last time with Chance Taker. A long time since she had been to bed with a man she cared about, and a man who cared about her needs.

Andrew Carter cared about her at that moment. He cared about her pleasure as he took her in long, slow strokes, making sure she was getting what she wanted, what she needed.

When she finally came, she closed her eyes and moaned aloud, and then she could feel him spurting inside of her, filling her with tiny hot needles . . .

"I'm sorry," he said, afterward.

"Don't be."

"It's been a long time for me."

"And for me."

He looked at her then as he sat on the edge of the bed, not touching her.

"You're very young, Liz."

"In some ways," she said. In other ways, she thought, she was not so young.

"I've got to go to work," he said, standing up and getting dressed. "You're welcome to stay as long as you like, Liz."

"I think I'll wait for Angie to get home," she said. "And then maybe I'll go into Paragon and stay for a few days. I hear it's a growing town."

"Fine."

"I'll be there for a while if you . . . want to talk."

"Fine," he said again.

He finished dressing and left.

Now, as she saddled Blossom and rode toward Paragon, Liz thought again about the suddenness of their coupling. It could have been good, she realized. It *had* been good. But it could have been even better if they had gone to bed with each other for the right reasons, instead of the wrong ones.

Maybe that was why she was going to Paragon — to see if he'd come to her for the right reasons.

Whatever they were . . .

Liz Archer's entry into Paragon did not go unnoticed. Although the tell-tale orange bandana was tucked inside her collar, her shimmering blonde hair attracted the eyes of both male and female onlookers.

Among them the eyes of James T. Morris.

Liz took Blossom down Paragon's main street, which was lined with horses and mules and travelled by buckboards and buggies, to the Paragon Livery. Then she walked to the Paragon Hotel. She knew that she was being watched, but that was all right. People were watching her because she was a beautiful woman, not because she was Angel Eyes. This was not conceit. She had long ago accepted her beauty as a fact, and in doing so had also accepted the attention she knew she would attract.

"I'd like a room, please," she said to the clerk, conscious of the young man's admiring stare.

"Yes, ma'am." He pushed the register over to her.

Liz thanked him when he gave her the key; then she ascended the stairs and found her room.

Staring out of her window, she studied the main street of Paragon, Wyoming. The town seemed busy, as befitted a place that was rapidly expanding. The street was thronged with people crossing, going to and from their jobs, and crowded with wagons filled with supplies of all types. This was a town where people should have been able to live as they liked. Yet wasn't it always towns like this that attracted men who felt they had a right to whatever they could take by force?

Men like James T. Morris.

During Angie's absence from the ranch — before Liz and Andrew had rather awkwardly and desperately made love — Andrew Carter had told her about Morris, how he had bought up most of the land surrounding the Carter ranch, buying it cheap from the bank after the owners couldn't make their payments, or finding some way to make the owners sell to him outright.

Why should a man like Morris be allowed to impose his will on people like Andrew and Angie Carter, people who were just trying to make a home for themselves.

The answer was easy.

He shouldn't.

CHAPTER SIX

"SHE'S IN TOWN." Morris told his men.

Morris was looking out his window when Liz Archer rode into town, and he had watched her with interest. She was a danger to him, it was true; but she was also a very beautiful woman, and he had not quite expected *that*. The recent stories about her dwelt more on her prowess with a gun than on her appearance.

He had no doubt that her beauty would soon be as legendary as her shooting — if she lived that long.

He was staring out the window now as Jack Tracy asked, "Angel Eyes?"

Morris turned slowly. "Who else would I mean?" he said, annoyed with the man's denseness.

"Then we can take care of her now." Tracy started for the door.

"Stand still, you fool." Morris said, wearily.

Tracy stopped short and stared at his boss, who lowered himself into the chair behind his desk. Morris smoothed his hair with both hands before continuing.

"I told you I've got Griff Taylor coming to town to take care of her."

"Yeah, but he won't be here for a couple of days, boss," Tracy said. "And she's here now."

"That's all right," Morris said. "She just got to town, and I have the feeling she won't be going anywhere for a while."

"What did she come to town for?" Lon asked, lisping through broken teeth and swollen lips. "Why ain't she staying out at the Carter ranch?"

"Who knows?" Morris said. "Maybe the young lady will come over and let us know."

"Maybe she came to town to kill you, boss," Tracy suggested.

"I doubt that," Morris said. "Not outright, anyway. Everybody in town knows I don't carry a gun, and I don't think she's going to shoot down an unarmed man. No, I think if she intends to do anything for the Carters, she might start by coming in for a talk."

"What do we do then?"

Morris shrugged and said, "We'll talk to her and see what she has to say."

"I ain't interested in anything she has to say," Jack Tracy declared.

"That's because you can't forget what she did to you," Morris said, rubbing his jaw thoughtfully. "Carter can't be paying her very much. Maybe I'll even be able to persuade her to change sides."

"We ain't working with her," Tracy said, remembering how she had embarrassed him and Lon. "Right, Lon?"

"Yeah, right."

"You won't have to," Morris said. "If I put her on my payroll it will only be until Griff Taylor gets here to deal with her."

"What do we do right now?" Tracy asked.

"Watch her," Morris said. "Just watch her. She's not so hard on the eyes, is she, Tracy?"

"She sure ain't."

As Tracy and Lon started for the door, Morris called out, "*Just* watch, Tracy. Maybe later I'll let you do more, but for now just keep an eye on her."

"Okay, boss," Tracy said. "Okay."

After his men left, Morris sat behind his desk, thinking things over and checking his own appearance in a hand mirror he kept in a drawer.

Tracy and Lon were wearing thin on him. He needed a better class of men working for him, because very soon he was going to be owner of all the land he could see. Maybe Griff Taylor would fill that bill.

He thought about Liz Archer then. He'd done some checking since discovering that she was Angel Eyes. She'd killed several men, and her fame was spreading. When people realized how beautiful she was, her fame would probably spread even faster.

He was almost sorry that he — through Griff Taylor's gun — was going to put an end to her rise to fame before it really got started.

CHAPTER SEVEN

AFTER ANGIE TOLD HER FATHER what had happened in town, Andrew Carter called for Ridge.

"You wanted to see me, Mr. Carter?" the foreman asked, as he entered the house.

Andrew Carter was seated at the kitchen table with a pot of coffee and two cups.

"Come in, Ridge. Have a cup of coffee."

"Thank you, sir."

Ridge sat and poured himself a cup, drinking it just the way it came out of the pot — hot and black.

"Angie told me what happened in town today."

"Yes sir."

"I appreciate what you did."

"It was my job."

"Your job is to run my ranch," Carter said. "To hire and fire. Not to risk yourself for my daughter."

"It's all the same."

Carter studied Ridge, examined the craggy, ugly face, the cold, expressionless eyes. He knew that the man seated across the table from him, though shorter then he in stature, had the strength to lift him by the throat off his feet with one hand and squeeze the life out of him. Ridge's strength was well known in these parts, which was more than could be said for the man himself. No one knew Ridge. Oh, Carter had known him for years, but he didn't really *know* him at all.

"How long have you worked for me, Ridge?"

"Since Angie was ten."

Carter frowned. He found the form of the answer odd. Ridge could have said, "For nine years," yet he had chosen to put it in terms of Angie's age.

"That's a long time."

"Yes, sir," Ridge said. He sipped the coffee, and the scalding heat of it did not seem to faze him.

"I'm going to give you a new responsibility, Ridge," Carter said.

"What's that, sir?"

"Until this thing with Morris is settled I want you to look out for Angie. Make sure no harm comes to her."

"The ranch — "

"I'll run the ranch," Carter said, interrupting the foreman. "You take care of Angie. Will you do that for me, Ridge?"

"Yes, sir. Nothing will happen to her."

"I know that, Ridge," Carter said. "I trust you."

"Will Angie know about this?"

"I'll tell her."

"All right."

Ridge finished his coffee and got up just as the door opened and Angie stepped in.

"Hello, Ridge."

"Miss Angie," Ridge said in passing.

When he was gone Angie looked at her father and asked, "Why does he always call me 'Miss Angie'? I've known him almost half my life."

"For the same reason he always calls me 'sir,' I suppose," her father answered. "Respect."

"I suppose. What were you two talking about?" she asked.

"You."

"Oh? What did he — "

"I called him in."

"What for?"

"I'm worried about you."

"I'll be all right, Pa," she said, putting her arms around her father's neck from behind. "Really."

"I'm just making sure."

"What do you mean?"

"From now on wherever you go, Ridge will go with you. He did a good job of protecting you this morning, so I've asked him to keep doing it."

"Really, Pa — "

"Now, don't argue. Until we've resolved our problem with Morris I don't want you to go anywhere alone."

"What about Liz. Why don't you hire her to watch after me?"

"Liz has already gone into town," he reminded her, shaking his head.

"We can ride in and ask her."

"What wrong with Ridge?"

Angie remembered the strange look in the foreman's eyes that morning and said, "Nothing, but I'd much rather have Liz around. Wouldn't you?"

Carter studied Angie for a moment, but the question seemed totally innocent.

"I don't think she would — "

"Can't I ask her? Ridge can ride into town with me so I can ask her."

"Angie — "

"Oh please, Pa," she asked, hugging his neck tightly.

Carter reached up to cover his daughter's hands with his and said, "Oh, all right. Ask her, but make sure you tell her that we can't pay much. She'll earn what the other hands earn."

"She won't care," Angie said, bounding toward the door happily. "I'll bet she'll do it for nothing. She likes us, you know."

"Really," Carter said, noncommitally.

"I'll tell Ridge right now so we can go and be back before dark."

"That's a good idea."

And having Liz around to watch over Angie was a better idea than he liked to admit to himself.

After leaving the house, Ridge went to the barn to be with the horses. In addition to his tremendous strength and his apparent disdain of friends, he was known for his ability to communicate with animals, particularly horses.

He often went to be with the horses when something was bothering him. It was virtually the only place where he was able to relax.

In this case what was bothering him was Angie Carter. "Little Angie." That was the way he used to think of her;

but he didn't think of her that way any more. He hadn't for some time now, and up to now he'd been able to conceal it.

Until the incident at the General Store.

He had seen it in Angie's eyes when he'd helped her to her feet, and he had immediately taken steps to hide it, but what did she think, now? She was so young. Was she able to recognize his feelings for what they were?

He hoped not.

"I don't know what I'd do then," he said to one of the horses, stroking the animal's nose.

That's where he was when Angie found him.

"Ridge?" she called from behind him.

Ride took a moment before turning to face her. She was prettier than he'd ever seen her before, like a young filly just starting to come into her full growth.

"Yes, Miss Angie?"

"My father told me what he told you. Could you saddle my horse, please? We're going into town."

"Yes, Miss Angie."

Angie turned and left the barn, and Ridge walked to her horse, rubbed its nose and said, "I just don't know."

CHAPTER EIGHT

ANGEL EYES SAW THEM RIGHT AWAY. Her Angel Eyes instincts were still working, even though she was trying to act more like just plain Liz Archer these days.

Of course. She had poked her nose into the business of Angie and Andrew Carter, and plain old Liz Archer's nose just wasn't going to be able to make the kind of impression that was necessary.

So she was Angel Eyes when she left her hotel room the next day, and although James Morris's men were trying to stay out of sight she spotted them.

Over breakfast she decided that they were just keeping an eye on her, and that was no reason to approach them. In fact, if an approach was made, it should probably be directly to the source, she thought. To Morris himself.

From everything Carter had told her about Morris she didn't think the simple fact of her presence would be enough to get him to leave the Carters alone.

Only some kind of action would make him back off, and that made her uneasy because she didn't know if she was ready to take that kind of action for the Carters. At least not yet.

She liked Angie well enough, and she had disturbing feelings toward Andrew Carter, but still . . .

She'd go and talk to Morris, she decided, and see what that accomplished. After that she'd just have to rethink the situation and see what else she was willing to do for people who were relative strangers to her.

When Liz Archer left the cafe and started across the street, Tracy and Lon started after her. Then both stopped short as they realized where she was headed.

"She's going to see the boss," Tracy said.

"What should we do?" Lon asked.

"We'll do what we were told to do, stupid," Tracy said. "We'll wait for her to come out and go on keeping an eye on her."

"Do you think the boss will really offer her a job?"

"If he does," Tracy said, "it's not going to help her a bit. She's going to pay for what she did to me — to us — in a big way."

When the knock came on James Morris's door he had a feeling he knew who it was. He smoothed his hair back and called out, "Come in."

He had seen the woman on the street from his window, but he still was not prepared for her stunning beauty.

"Mr. Morris?"

He was staring at her, and he started when she said his name aloud.

"Uh, yes. Can I help you?"

"I think you can," Liz said, closing the office door and approaching Morris's desk. "My name is Liz Archer."

"Should I know who you are?"

Liz decided to let that go by and said, "That really doesn't matter. I'm just a friend of Andrew and Angie Carter."

"I see. How can I help you, Miss Archer?"

"I'd like to talk to you about them."

"About who?"

"The Carters."

Morris shrugged his shoulders as if the subject held no interest for him at all. "What about them?"

"They're very happy with their lives the way they are," Liz said. Then she added, "And with *where* they are."

"That's nice," Morris said. "Everyone should be able to say that."

"Can you?"

Morris was studying Liz with interest, the kind of interest a man has in a beautiful woman. He could think of something that would make him extremely happy at that moment. To take off that gun she was wearing on her lean hips — very unfeminine, that — and then to take those pants off . . .

"Not all the time."

"Why do you need so much land, Mr. Morris?"

"Why don't you call me James, Miss Archer?"

"Mr. Morris," she said again, rather pointedly, "why do you need the land that the Carter ranch is on?"

Morris didn't say anything, but at that moment Liz noticed a map on the wall behind him that answered her question. It was a map of the country around Paragon, Wyoming, with various plots of land shaded in. The Carter ranch, unshaded, stood out clearly. It appeared to be almost an oasis in the center of James Morris's land holdings.

Morris sensed where she was looking and glanced back over his shoulder at the map.

"My holdings," he said.

"You have a lot of land," Liz observed, and then asked, "Why do you want more?"

"Everyone wants more, Miss Archer," James Morris answered. "No matter how much they have."

"Not everyone."

There was a moment of silence, and then Morris said, "Is that all you wanted to talk about?"

"Unless we're both prepared to speak a little plainer," she said.

"How do you mean?"

"I like the Carters, Mr. Morris. I wouldn't want to see their land taken away from them."

"And you think I'm going to do that?"

"I think you're going to try. In fact, I think you have been trying."

"All the land I own I obtained by legal means," Morris said, jerking his thumb behind him to indicate the map. "What makes you think I would go outside the law now?"

"The Carters don't want to sell."

"Make someone the right offer and they'll sell."

"Not these people."

"What makes them so special?"

"I . . . don't know."

"Look, Miss Archer. I've made repeated offers to those people for their land and they've said no, so I'll just keep making offers until they say yes. That's how I do business. That's how I became a success."

"What about your men?"

"My men?"

"Tracy and his partner."

"What about them?"

"You had nothing to do with them going after Angie Carter?"

"Going after her?"

"And they would have gotten her if I hadn't dealt myself in."

"Oh," Morris said, raising his eyebrows. "Now I know who you are. My men told me about that incident, Miss Archer. They weren't 'after' her as you put it. They were simply going in the same direction."

"Sure."

"There was really no cause for you to do what you did, either. You embarrassed them badly."

"They'll live," Liz said.

"You also impressed *me* greatly," Morris said. "So much so that I'd like to make you an offer."

"Such as?"

"I'm tired of having second-raters like Tracy and Lon in my employ. I'd like to replace them."

"With me?"

He nodded and said, "Yes, with you."

"And what makes you think I'm not a second-rater?" she asked.

"Because I know who you are."

"Oh, really? When I came in, you asked why my name should mean anything to you."

"It popped into my mind, like an inspiration," Morris said, waving his hands in the air like a magician.

"All right, then, who am I?"

"You're Angel Eyes, the lady with the fast gun."

"And the gun is not for hire."

This visit was a mistake, she knew; she had known it almost as soon as she walked into the office.

"Look, why don't we take this conversation out of my office and continue it over dinner this evening?" Morris said, touching his right eyebrow with his forefinger. "I'm sure I can convince you that I am not as bad a person as you apparently think I am."

"I'm afraid not."

"I really would like to see what you're like without that gun, Miss Archer," Morris said, turning on what even Liz admitted was considerable charm. Unfortunately for Morris, it was lost on her.

"First you want my gun, and now you don't. You should make up your mind, Mr. Morris."

He studied her for a moment, speculatively, then said, "I think I'd much rather know you without your gun."

She walked to the door, opened it and said, "That's something that you'd never be able to make me a good enough offer for, Mr. Morris." Then she walked out, leaving James Morris to smooth his hair and frown.

CHAPTER NINE

AS LIZ ARCHER came out of Morris's office, Tracy and Lon backed into a doorway, out of sight. They watched her cross the street.

"She don't look happy," Lon said.

"Good," Tracy said, staring at her with eyes that seemed to be burning.

Someone else saw her come out, too.

"There's Liz," Angie Carter said to Ridge as they were dismounting.

"I see her."

Angie frowned when she realized what building Liz had come out of.

"Ridge?"

"Yeah?"

"That building she came out of."

"What about it?"

"Isn't that where Morris has his office?"

"Yes."

Angie frowned and wondered aloud what Liz could have been doing with James Morris.

"Only one way you're gonna find out," Ridge said, and Angie knew what that was.

As Liz approached the saloon she saw Angie coming from the opposite direction. Beyond Angie she could see the foreman, Ridge, standing stolidly across the street, watching.

"Hello, Angie."

"I came to town to talk to you."

"And Ridge?"

Angie turned and looked at the man, then back to Liz. "Pa wants him to look after me," she said.

"How do you feel about that?"

"I made another suggestion to Pa."

"What was that?" Liz asked, although she was pretty sure she could guess.

"That we hire you to watch me," Angie said. Hurriedly she added, "It's just until Pa can figure out a way to keep Morris off our backs."

"I see."

"Will you do it?"

"Angie — "

"We'll pay you."

"That's not the problem, Angie."

"Then, what is it?" Angie asked, frowning. "I thought you liked us."

Angie was on the verge of womanhood, but in some ways she was still a child.

"That's not the point, either, Angie."

"Then what is?"

Liz paused, and Angie looked across the street at the building where James Morris had his office.

"Did Morris make you a better offer?" the young girl suddenly asked.

"Angie — "

"That's it, isn't it?" Angie said. "Morris asked you to work for him."

"No, he didn't."

"Liz, we need your help," Angie said. "Pa won't admit it, but we do. We need help."

All of a sudden, Liz felt silly standing there in front of the saloon discussing this with Angie.

"Angie, I'll come and talk to your father about it."

"Now?"

"Not right now," Liz said. "I've got to do some thinking, first."

"Later, then?"

"Yes," Liz said. "Later."

"I'll tell him."

Angie turned and, like a little girl, trotted across the street to where Ridge was waiting.

Since she was already in front of the saloon, Liz decided to do her thinking over a drink. She knew that Tracy and Lon were behind her, and that Morris was probably watching her from his window. The visit had accomplished nothing, except to give her a bad taste in her mouth about James Morris. He was too slick and full of himself for her — the kind of man who thought anything he wanted should be his for the asking, or the buying — or the taking.

He needed to be taught a lesson, but Liz still had to work out whether she was the one to teach it to him.

She watched Angie mount up and ride out of town with Ridge, then went into the saloon for a much-needed drink.

CHAPTER TEN

LIZ WAS ALMOST DONE with her beer when the man with the badge walked through the bat-wing doors. It took only a moment for her to realize that he was looking for her.

It took him less time than that to spot her.

In fact, all of the men in the room had their eyes on her, and she had put up with it even longer than usual. It had become her habit to have one beer and then leave, before the male eyes in the place developed hands.

The sheriff reached her table just as she drained the last of the beer.

"Miss Archer?"

"That's right."

He was a tall, slender man in his mid-thirties with intense blue eyes and an even more intense look on his face. She sensed that he wasn't looking at her the way the other men in the room were.

"I'd like to talk to you, if I may."

"About what?"

"Can I sit down?"

"I was just about to leave."

"It'll only take a moment."

"All right," she said. "But don't you think you'd better introduce yourself?"

"I'm sorry," the lawman said, sitting down opposite her. "My name is Bateman — Sheriff Peter Bateman."

"Liz Archer."

"I know," Bateman said. "Angel Eyes."

Liz let that pass. She knew the sheriff couldn't have recognized her. Her reputation had not spread that far, yet. Someone had to have told him who she was, and she had a pretty good idea who had done it.

"Could we get right to the point, Sheriff?"

"Sure," Bateman said. "I'd prefer it that way. Truth of the matter is, I'm a little nervous about having an up-and-coming legend in my town."

"I don't find that amusing."

The sheriff stared at her for a moment, then his face relaxed.

"I'm sorry. Maybe I'm wrong."

"Maybe you are."

"But you must admit that you do have something of a reputation."

"I didn't go after it," she said. "But I refuse to run away from it, either."

"That's fine, Miss Archer. I'm just anxious to keep trouble out of my town."

"It didn't ride in with me," she assured him, "in spite of what you might have heard."

"Will you be staying in Paragon long?"

"I don't know."

"Why did you come?"

"I'm visiting friends," she said, without hesitation.

"You didn't come here in response to an offer of employment?"

"The only offer of employment I've had lately is one I just received from a man named James Morris," she said, deciding that since Angie's offer had not come from the head of the Carter family she wouldn't count it. "I turned him down."

"What did Mr. Morris want you to do?" Bateman asked, frowning.

"I didn't ask him," Liz said, standing up. "Maybe you should. Is that all, Sheriff?"

Bateman stood up and said, "Just one more thing, Miss Archer. I'd appreciate it if you'd check in with me before you shoot anyone."

"That's not f — " she started to protest, but Bateman turned and walked out before she could let him know just how unfair that was.

As she rode out of Paragon toward the Carter ranch she wasn't sure who she was more angry at, James Morris or Sheriff Peter Bateman.

"Liz is coming out to talk to you," Angie Carter told her father.

"About what?" Andrew Carter asked.

Angie had found her father at the corral, checking over a couple of strays to make sure they hadn't injured themselves.

"About working for us."

"She said that?"

"Not exactly."

"Angie," Carter said, leaning on a fencepost and mopping his brow, "what did she say?"

"She said that before she decided she'd have to come out and talk to you."

"All right," he said. "If she comes out, we'll talk."

He had already turned back to his work when Angie said, "Well, get ready to talk."

Carter spun around as Angie added, "Because here she comes."

"Liz. Over here!" Angie called, as Liz rode up to the house and dismounted.

"Angie," Andrew Cater said quickly, "why don't you go and ask Ridge if there are any more strays in that valley?"

"But Pa, you were there yourself. You know these are the only — "

"Angie," he said, cutting her off. "Go ask Ridge if he was looking for me."

She opened her mouth to argue but suddenly realized that her father wanted to talk to Liz without her around.

"All right, Pa."

As Liz approached the corral Angie trotted past her with a quick, "Hi!"

"Where is she off to in such an all-fired hurry?" Liz asked Carter.

"I figured it would be easier for us to talk without her here," Carter explained. "I don't want you to feel any pressure about this."

"About what?"

"About taking on the job of looking after my Angie for me."

It was the first time Liz had heard Andrew Carter refer to his daughter as "my" Angie, and she thought it sounded just fine.

"I don't think I'll be taking the job, Andrew."

"I see. Well, that's all right. Ridge is perfectly capable of — "

"I'll do it for nothing."

"For nothing?" he asked, surprised. "Liz, I can't ask you to — "

"You're not asking me," Liz said. "I have my reasons for doing this."

"What are they?"

"I like Angie."

"And?"

"Fishing for compliments?" she asked, grinning at him.

"No. I just don't think that's a particularly good reason for someone to take on a job for free."

"All right, then. I went to talk to James Morris today."

"And?"

"He wanted me to go to work for him."

"Doing what?" Carter asked, frowning.

"I didn't ask, I just turned him down. He did manage to make me dislike him, though, and that's another reason I'm taking your job for free."

"Are there any others?"

Liz thought about Sheriff Bateman and said, "Maybe, but I think I'll keep some of my reasons to myself, if that's all right with you."

"I suppose you're entitled," Carter agreed, after a moment.

"Thanks."

"I guess that means you'll be coming back out here after only one day in town?"

Liz had thought about that on the way. She had another idea that she thought might work.

"Andrew, you're afraid that Angie might get hurt if Morris's men come out here some night, right?"

"Either that or they'll simply grab her."

"How about letting her come into town and stay there with me?"

"Town?" Carter asked. "She'd be closer to Morris than ever, then."

"That may be," Liz said. "But she'd also be close to the sheriff."

"Bateman," Carter said, and Liz thought she detected some hidden emotion in the word.

"He strikes me as a serious lawman," Liz said. "Do you know something I don't?"

"Like what?"

"Like, is he working for Morris?"

"I don't know," Carter said. "I don't like Morris, but I won't make a judgement like that against him without some sort of evidence."

"Let me ask you this, then," Liz said. "How long do you think it will be before you can work out this land thing with Morris?"

"I don't know if I can," Carter muttered unhappily. "But I am going to try to reason with the man."

"Like I said," Liz replied, "I met the man today. I wish you luck."

Carter came out of the corral and they both started walking back to the house together.

"Well, I guess I might as well say what I'm thinking," Carter said as they reached the porch.

"Which is?"

"I'm glad you're . . . not leaving."

"I'll do my best to keep her safe, Andrew," Liz said, taking hold of Blossom's reins.

"That's not what I meant," Carter said as she mounted up.

She smiled down at him and said, "I know." Then she went to find Angie.

CHAPTER ELEVEN

JAMES MORRIS was concerned.

He was concerned about the fact that a stunningly beautiful woman — Liz Archer — had not responded even a little to his charm. Morris did not enjoy doubting his appeal to the opposite sex, so he left his office and went to the little white house he maintained for Sarah Medford, his "mistress."

"This is an early visit for you, James," Sarah said.

Feeling a need to reassert his hold over Sarah, he said harshly, "That's what I pay you for, Sarah. To be ready when I want you."

"That's cruel," she said. "You're hardly ever cruel, unless — "

"Unless what?" he demanded.

Sarah thought better of reminding Morris that he was only cruel when a woman had rebuffed him. It was as if he had to come to her then to reaffirm that he had something — beyond the money and power he held — that women wanted.

"What?" he asked.

"Nothing."

"Then get undressed."

Sarah Meford was thirty-nine, a lovely, statuesque brunette who was convinced that her figure was becoming matronly. Because of this she would take whatever James Morris dished out. He gave her money and a place to live, and he made her feel desirable — at times. It was those times she waited for; it was for those times that she withstood his occasional harsh treatment.

They were two of a kind, both in their late thirties, concerned about their approaching forties, fearful of losing their youth and reaching for each other whenever they needed to convince themselves they were still young.

Having Sarah at his beck and call also saved Morris the ignominy of having to patronize the local whorehouse.

And so there they were, both naked, Sarah's large breasts sagging slightly, Morris's paunch just a bit too pronounced.

"You're beautiful," he said.

"So are you," she said.

They closed on each other, encircling each other with their arms. Sarah's distended nipples rubbed against Morris's chest while his erect penis poked her in the belly.

"James," she said, taking hold of his rigid cock.

"Yes."

"I want you."

"Yes."

"In my mouth."

"Yes."

The words were the same ones they always used.

She fell to her knees, nuzzled the spongy, swollen head of his erection with her cheek, and then opened her full-lipped mouth to take him inside.

''Yes,'' he hissed as she began to suck on him while cupping his hanging testicles.

She reached behind him to cup his buttocks, digging into them with her nails as she continued to suck.

''Enough,'' he said when he felt he wouldn't be able to take any more.

Obediently, she released him, stood up, and walked to the bed where she lay down on her back and spread her long legs wide.

Morris approached the bed and settled on it between her spread legs, his face buried in her crotch. His tongue poked through the tangle of her pubic bush, lapping at her sweetness, flicking at her clit.

''Oh, yes, James,'' she murmured, cupping the back of his head. ''Yes, yes, yes.''

He felt her belly begin to tremble and closed his lips over her straining clit. At that moment she came, straining up off the bed as her body was wracked by her orgasm.

Morris got to his knees then, positioned himself and rammed his cock into her forcefully, piercing her in mid-orgasm so that her second started even before the first had ended.

''Oh, God,'' she cried out, wrapping her legs tightly around his waist. He continued to drive himself into her, enjoying the power he was experiencing, the power he always experienced when he was between a woman's legs.

He could stop now, he knew, and she'd beg him to continue.

That was real power!

Only he didn't want to stop. He wanted to go on and on,

listening to her harsh breathing, her moans, even her screams, until he was finally emptying into her, ejaculating with a force that was almost painful.

Take that, Liz Archer, he thought, closing his eyes and straining. Take that, Angel Eyes . . .

"Who were you thinking of?" she asked afterward, watching him dress.

"No one."

"Of course."

"Don't ask me any questions, Sarah."

"I need some money."

"Of course you do."

When he'd finished dressing he took out his wallet, removed some large bills and laid them neatly on the dresser without looking at her.

He left without saying goodbye.

When Morris crossed paths with Sheriff Bateman he was still feeling his oats from his visit with Sarah Medford.

"Bateman."

The sheriff looked at the other man and nodded. "Mr. Morris."

"Did you get a chance to speak with the woman?"

"Liz Archer?"

"Who else?" Morris said shortly.

"Yes, I spoke to her."

Morris waited and when there was no further response he said, "And?"

"She doesn't appear to be here to start any kind of trouble."

"So she says," Morris replied. "She's got a reputation, you know."

"I know all about her reputation, Mr. Morris," Bateman said. "I checked her out. She tracked down some men who killed her family and . . . took care of most of them."

"Does she have a price on her head?"

"No."

Morris looked annoyed.

"She said that you offered her a job."

"I did no such thing," Morris said. "She lied. That alone should indicate that she has something to hide."

"Maybe," Bateman said. "If she lied."

"Are you doubting my word?"

"No."

"You'd be wise to remember who I am, Bateman," Morris said to the lawman.

"Is there anything else I can do for you?" the sheriff asked.

"No," Morris said, and then, quickly, "Yes."

Bateman waited patiently, aware of the power that James Morris wielded in Paragon. It annoyed him, but he waited anyway.

"Keep an eye on her."

"Why does she have you worried?"

"Just keep an eye on her, Bateman, that's all," Morris said. "Don't question me."

"I've got my own duties to perform, Morris," Bateman said, unable to conceal his growing annoyance. "Part of that is keeping an eye on strangers."

"Fine."

"But you've already got two men watching her," Bateman went on. "Tracy and Lon. I've told her not to start any trouble; now I'm telling you the same thing."

"Who do you think — "

"Just pass the word on to Tracy," Bateman interrupted.

"He's your man and I'm going to hold you responsible for him."

"And I think the town council is going to have to hold you responsible as well, Sheriff," Morris said in a threatening tone. "There will be a meeting called very soon. You can count on it."

"I'll be there."

Angie liked the idea of going into Paragon to stay with Liz.

"We'll be like sisters, almost."

"Almost," Liz agreed. "But you're going to have to do as I say, Angie."

"You mean listen to you as I listen to Pa?"

"No," Andrew Carter said, entering the barn where Liz had been watching as Angie saddled her horse.

"Pa."

"Listen to me, young lady," Carter said. "You do whatever Liz tells you without question, do you hear? You pay her *more* mind than you pay me — which God knows is very little."

"Pa," Angie said, approaching her father and hugging him. "You know I'm stubborn like Ma was. You always say that."

"Your mother knew when to listen, Angie," Andrew Carter said. "I hope that you have that part of her in you, too."

"Don't worry, Pa."

Carter looked at Liz and said, "I've still got some strays to round up, but tomorrow I'll be coming into town to talk to Morris."

"About what?" Angie asked curiously.

"Maybe there's a way we can settle this, Angie, without somebody getting hurt."

"It's just like you, Pa," Angie said, "to think that you could talk to a man like Morris."

"I'm willing to give it a try, honey."

"That's more than *he's* willing to do."

"That may be, but I've got to make the attempt."

"Will you let me know what happens?"

Carter nodded and said, "Right after I finish talking to him."

"All right, Angie," Liz said, deciding to test Angie's obedience from the outset. "Let's finish saddling up and get moving."

Angie glanced over at her father, then moved to finish saddling the animal. Liz and Andrew exchanged mildly satisfied glances.

Neither one held out much hope for total obedience, but this was a start.

Tracy and Lon had followed Liz Archer to the Carter ranch, keeping her in sight without getting too close. Now they were watching from the same cautious distance.

"Maybe we should get closer," Lon suggested, squinting as he peered toward the Carter ranch. His speech had cleared up some, but he still sounded mush-mouthed.

"Why?"

"To hear what's going on."

"We don't have to hear," Tracy said, staring intently at the Carter barn. "Our orders are to watch, and that's what we'll do."

Watch, Tracy thought, and wait.

CHAPTER TWELVE

WHEN PETE BATEMAN RETURNED to his office after the conversation with James Morris, his deputy, Sam Rogers, noticed that something was bothering him.

"Problem, Pete?"

Bateman looked at the young deputy and said, "Trouble brewing, Sam, and I don't like the smell of it."

"What kind of trouble?"

"The worst kind," Bateman said, sitting down behind his desk. "We got a man with money who thinks he can buy anything — "

"Morris," Rogers offered.

" — and we got a pretty lady who wears a gun and has a reputation for knowing how to use it."

"Who's that?"

"Angel Eyes."

"I've heard of her," Rogers said. "She cleaned up on the Nolans pretty good, didn't she?"

"She did."

"Why do you think she's here?"

"Damned if I know," Bateman said. "But if she's not working for Morris then she's working against him, and that spells trouble."

"You think Tracy and Lon can handle her?"

"No, I don't," Bateman said. "And that's what worries me. Morris knows they can't handle her, either."

"Which means he'll bring in somebody else."

"Somebody with a rep," Bateman added. "And a well-deserved one. That's the kind of trouble we don't need in Paragon, Sam. The kind where somebody ends up dead!"

Griff Taylor never worked without back-up.

Not that the gunman didn't have supreme confidence in his own abilities; but he had learned in the army — during the war — that it was wise to have someone with you when going into battle.

And so, on his way to Paragon, he stopped off to pick up his back-up.

John the Beast.

"You've heard of John the Baptist?" the naked man asked the naked prostitute.

"Yes."

"Well, I'm John the Beast."

"I can see why," the girl said, eyeing him with pleasure.

She was staring between his legs, where a penis the size of a tree jutted — and the rest of the man was just as huge. His shoulders sloped into arms that were corded with hard muscles, and his thighs were like tree trunks.

"Come here," John told the girl. He had picked the biggest girl he could find in the Coleman's Bend, Wyoming, bordello. As she approached him her large breasts swayed gently, and he reached out with his massive hands to grasp them.

Just then the door to the room opened and Griff Taylor stepped in.

"Beast?" he said, his tone — and his familiar voice — drawing the man's attention away from the girl.

John the Beast turned and looked at Taylor.

"Aw, Griff," he said with unconcealed disappointment.

"We've got work," Taylor said, eyeing the tall, full-bodied girl appreciatively.

"Can't it wait?"

The girl was easily five-ten, maybe more—a young girl with huge firm breasts that would always be huge but would not always be firm. From where he was standing Griff Taylor could smell her bitch-in-heat scent, and he couldn't help but respond to it.

Still, technically, he was working, and he didn't indulge in whores while he was working.

"Sorry, Beast."

John the Beast looked at the girl with a sorrowful look on his face and said, "Sorry, girlie."

"Come on, honey," she replied, not quite ready to give up the biggest man she'd ever seen. Moving close to him she grasped his massive manhood with both hands and said, "Who's he, anyway? He can't give you what I got for you."

She moved closer still and started rubbing her breasts against his chest, and for a moment John the Beast looked as if he might cry.

Then he pushed her away at arm's length and backhanded her effortlessly, sending her flying across the room with a split cheek.

Taylor waited while the Beast dressed. The girl lay semi-conscious on the bed.

"She's going to be one mad bitch when she wakes up," he told the big man.

"That's what she gets for opening her mouth for something other than sucking," the Beast said.

"She never would have been able to fit it, anyway," Taylor laughed.

"Now we'll never know," the Beast said mournfully. "Who we gonna kill this time?"

"We'll find that out when we get where we're going."

"Which is?"

"Paragon."

"Never been there."

"Well we better get started before this bitch wakes up and starts screaming to bring the whole house down on us," Taylor said.

"I'm ready," the man known as John the Beast said. "Somebody in Paragon is gonna to have to pay for me losing out on that," he added, indicating the naked girl on the bed. "Somebody's gonna have to pay real bad."

Griff Taylor felt sorry for his next target if John the Beast got his hands on him first.

That person would be better off dead.

As darkness approached, Angie and Liz Archer rode toward Paragon with Tracy and Lon still on their tail.

"Do you know we're being followed?" Angie asked Liz as they approached town. Liz's respect for the young woman went up a notch.

"*I'm* being followed," Liz corrected her. "I have been ever since I talked to Morris."

"Should we do something about it?"

"Yes."

"What?" the younger woman asked anxiously. "Double back and come up behind them? Wait for them somewhere further on? Or should we — "

"None of that," Liz said, cutting Angie's eager words off.

"Then what?"

"We'll do what they're doing, Angie."

"What's that?"

"We'll just wait."

CHAPTER THIRTEEN

LIZ ARCHER HAD a dream that night.

A two-part dream.

The first part was good . . .

She was with Tate Gilmore again, as they had been together that first night when she had first made love with him . . . or with any man, for that matter.

Tate's arms were around her, his mouth was on her, sucking her nipples into rigid little turrets, moving lower on her body until he was licking her navel, and then darting his tongue through the tangle of her pubic hair and touching the core of her being, untouched until then.

He had brought her alive, and she was once again experiencing the sensations of awakening to what it meant to be a woman, a fulfilled woman . . .

And then the second part of the dream started . . .

Liz was with Chance Taker, the gambler who had possessed her heart for the first time, as Tate had possessed her body.

Chance was kissing her and she felt dizzy, because not just her senses but her emotions had been awakened by this man, and she was feeling strange new sensations. As if his mouth and hands were caressing her heart and soul, as well as her body.

And that's when the dream went wrong . . .

She was standing off at a distance, watching the action as if through a haze, a fog . . .

Chance sat at a poker table across from a lone man, and suddenly the other man leaped to his feet and drew his gun. The look on Chance's face was one of surprise, shock . . . and fear!

The other man's gun went off and, in slow motion, Liz watched the bullet enter Chance's chest. Red blossomed forth in an unstoppable torrent, and she tried unsuccessfully to rush to his aid.

It was as if her feet were mired in quicksand!

She watched helplessly as Chance fell to the floor and the other man turned to leave.

She tried to shout at him to wait, to turn around and face her, but her voice would not come. The man was leaving and she couldn't stop him, unless . . .

She reached for her gun, closing her hand on the butt. That was as far as she got, because the gun wouldn't come out of her holster.

She pulled harder, but it wouldn't budge.

The man had killed Chance, and there had been nothing she could do to stop him. Now he was leaving and there was nothing she could do to stop that, either.

Suddenly, her feet were free to move, as if the quicksand had disappeared, and she rushed to Chance's side, cradled his head in her lap and cried . . .

"*Liz*!"

She heard her name and suddenly came awake.

"What?"

She sat up abruptly in bed and tried to remember where she was.

"Are you all right?"

She looked down at the floor where Angie lay in her bedroll. She remembered that they had come to the room together and argued over who would get the bed, and she had finally given into the younger woman's logic that it was Liz's room, so the bed was hers.

"Angie."

"Are you all right?" Angie asked again.

Liz realized that her face was wet with tears and angrily wiped them away with the back of her hand. She had not dreamed about Chance for a long time, and this had been a bad time to do so, with Angie in the room.

"I'm fine."

"You were crying."

"It was just a dream."

"Want to talk about it?"

"No."

"Best way to get rid of a bad dream is to talk about it," Angie insisted. "My ma taught me that."

After a moment's pause Liz said, "We'd better get back to sleep, Angie."

Angie apparently accepted Liz's resistance to discussing her dream and said, "All right," in a tone that was more disappointed than hurt.

It was quiet for a few minutes, as if both women had gone back to sleep. Then Liz said, "Maybe in the morning, all right?"

"What?"

"Maybe in the morning," she said again, "we can talk about it."

"All right," Angie said again, sounding happier. "Goodnight, Liz."

" 'Night, Angie."

Liz lay down in bed and turned on her side so that her back was to Angie. She wiped the last of the tears away, still angry at having cried, at having cried with Angie in the room. She turned the pillow over so that the tear-stained spot was underneath.

She didn't sleep much the rest of the night.

CHAPTER FOURTEEN

THE FOLLOWING MORNING — early — Andrew Carter arrived at James Morris's office. Whether it was going to work or not, he wanted to get the meeting over with. Being in Morris's presence was always distasteful to him.

He knocked on Morris's door and immediately regretted it. It might have put him at a disadvantage; he probably should have barged right in. But then . . . that might have been the wrong move, too.

Ah, hell . . .

"Come in."

"Morris," Carter said as he entered.

"Well," Morris said, smiling. "Mr. Andrew Carter. Come to accept my last offer?"

"I can't even remember what it was," Carter said as he approached the man's desk.

"Oh? What brings you here, then?"

"I want to talk to you about my ranch."

"You want to make me an offer?"

"Sort of."

"You don't say?" Morris said, folding his hands in front of him. "I'm curious. Please, sit down."

"I wonder when Pa will come to town?" Angie asked Liz over breakfast.

"He may already be here."

"Maybe we should go and — "

"Stay where you are and have your coffee."

Angie looked disappointed, then picked up her post-breakfast coffee cup.

"Want to talk about last night?" she asked.

Looking uncomfortable, Liz said, "It was just a bad dream."

"You said that last night."

"It was still a bad dream."

"You said we'd talk about it in the morning."

"I said maybe."

"That's not fair."

Liz studied Angie for a few seconds and then relented.

"No," she said. "I guess maybe it isn't."

"That's your offer?" Morris asked, looking amused.

"Yes."

"That I be satisfied with the land I've got and leave yours alone?"

"What's wrong with that?" Carter asked. "Look at that map, Morris."

"I don't have to look at it," Morris said. "I have it memorized."

"You've got most of the land around me — "

"I've got all of the land that directly borders yours, Carter."

"Then why do you need mine? We can co-exist, Morris. It's not impossible."

"Yes," Morris said. "It is impossible, Mr. Carter."

"Why?"

"Because I want your land," the other man said. "I want it."

Carter's face grew red and he stood up abruptly.

"I'll fight you!"

"You've already started, haven't you?" Morris asked calmly.

Carter frowned and said, "What do you mean?"

"You've hired yourself a gun."

"You don't mean . . . Liz Archer?"

Morris nodded and said, "Better known as Angel Eyes."

"I haven't hired her to be a . . . a gun fighter," Carter said.

"That's not what your daughter said."

"Angie?"

"At least once that I know of she's said that Angel Eyes works for you."

"Liz is only watching over my daughter, keeping her safe from your gunnies."

"Tracy and Lon? They're not my gunnies," Morris said, looking well satisfied with himself.

"Hard cases, then."

"They're hardly hard enough to handle your man Ridge, let alone Angel Eyes," Morris admitted. "No, I've got something else in mind entirely."

"What do you mean?"

"I mean you've hired Angel Eyes, and I've hired . . . someone." Morris leaned forward and said, "Let the best gun win."

"This is crazy."

"It may be crazy, Carter," Morris said, "but it's also almost over."

"That's sad," Angie said after Liz finished telling her about Chance Taker.

"Well, it taught me something," Liz said. "I've got to watch out for the one person who means the most to me in the world."

"Who?"

"Me."

Angie seemed to think about that for a moment, then looked at Liz and said, "That's sad, too."

Andrew Carter found them in the cafe. He looked agitated.

"We have to talk," he said, pulling a chair away from another table so he could sit with them.

"Did you talk to Morris already?" Angie asked anxiously.

"I did," he said, glaring at her. "Angie, did you tell anyone that we had taken Liz on as a hired gun?"

"I, uh — "

"Tell me the truth, young lady," her father warned.

"I, uh, might have mentioned it to — "

"It doesn't matter who you mentioned it to."

"What's wrong, Andrew?" Liz asked.

Carter looked at her and said, "Morris thinks I've hired your gun, so he's hired one for himself."

"Who?"

"I don't know, but he seemed pretty smug about it."

"Did you tell him that you hadn't actually hired me?"

"I tried to tell him, Carter said. "The trouble is I lost my temper and told him I'd fight him. He figured my first move was to hire you."

"Well, you haven't," Liz said angrily. "Not for my gun, anyway. I don't hire my gun out."

"Don't get mad at us," Angie said, touching her father's arm protectively.

Liz started to answer, "Why not?" but checked herself. True, the problem was theirs, but her involvement was not their fault; it was hers. She had taken a hand that first day, and everything had stemmed from that.

Her presence had actually escalated the confrontation into what it was now—or what it was in danger of becoming unless she did something to stop it.

Like leave town.

"I'll have to leave."

"What?" said Angie, startled.

"It's the only way," Liz went on. "If his gun shows up and I'm gone, there won't be any work for him."

"He'll come after us," Angie said, tightening her grip on her father's arm.

"No, he won't," Liz said. "He'll be too expensive for Morris to keep around just to take care of you. Tracy, Lon and a few others could do that."

"There's Ridge," Carter said.

"What about Ridge?" Liz asked anxiously. "He seems more than capable."

"He is," Carter said. "But he's a strange one. I believe I can count on him, but I . . . I can't be completely sure about him."

"Well," Liz said, "I still think the best thing for me to do is leave."

"Why don't you talk to Morris," Angie asked, "and explain it to him?"

"He won't believe me."

"You can try."

"I don't think he'll listen, Angie," Carter said, touching his daughter's hand. "We don't have any right to ask her to stay and get involved with our troubles. If she wants to leave, let her go." Andrew Carter looked at Liz then and added, "There won't be any hard feelings."

Liz looked first at Carter, then at Angie. The expressions on their faces had one thing in common: they were pitiful.

"Oh hell," she said, standing up. "So *I'll* try talking to him."

CHAPTER FIFTEEN

"FIRST YOUR BOSS. And now you," Morris commented as Liz entered his office without knocking. "You going to shoot me?"

"He's not my boss, damn it!" she snapped, striding up to the man's desk until she bumped into it.

"Why are you here, then?"

"I'm here to try and keep you from making a serious mistake, Morris," she said. "Do you want that little patch of land enough to spill blood over it?"

"Carter brought a hired gun in first."

"I am not a hired gun!"

"You'll have a hard time convincing me of that, young lady," Morris said. Then, smugly, he added, "I've checked you out thoroughly. You have quite a little reputation going for yourself. Are you telling me you have no desire to add to it?"

"None at all," Liz said. "And if I did, I wouldn't add to it by going against you."

"Ah, but against a man of my choosing," Morris replied. "And I stress the word 'man.' "

"If you bring in a hired gun you're going to turn this into a war." Liz brought her hands down flat on the desk top with a bang and added, "Be reasonable, man."

"Tell that to your boss," Morris said. "I've made him a good offer for his land."

"You're trying to buy a man's home."

"He can find another one."

"Morris —"

"I think you'll be very interested to find out who I've hired, Miss Angel Eyes," he interrupted. "Very interested, indeed."

"I couldn't care less," she told him. "And if you don't listen to reason, I won't be here to see who it is."

"You planning on leaving town?" he asked. "That won't do your reputation any good."

"I don't care," Liz said. "I'm trying to find a way to stop bloodshed."

"Leaving town won't stop it."

"No?"

"No. If you're not here when my man arrives, I'll send him after Carter."

"That'd be murder!"

"And then after his daughter."

"Why?" she demanded. "Why would you do something like that?"

"Because I want that land," Morris said with a smile. "I want all the land I can get my hands on."

"And you're willing to kill for it?"

"I repeat," Morris said patiently, "that I was not the

first to bring in a hired gun — and you can spare me your protestations, Miss Angel Eyes. They wouldn't be calling you that — or some other equally ridiculous name — if you hadn't earned it with your gun. Whether you want to or not,'' he finished, ''you're going to have to live up to it.''

She started for the door, but before she went through it she heard him add, ''Or die trying.''

Liz Archer stalked angrily across the street to the cafe where she'd left Andrew and Angie Carter. She did not see the two men who had just turned their horses onto Paragon's main street.

''This is Paragon?'' John the Beast asked Griff Taylor.

''This it it.''

''Don't seem like much.''

''We ain't getting paid to like it here,'' Taylor said. ''Just to do a job.''

''Well, I hope we get to do it quick.''

''John,'' Griff Taylor said in a gently scolding tone, ''you know I never do anything quick.''

''Griff,'' John the Beast said, and his tone was one of warning, ''if I don't get me a woman soon —''

''You'll just get meaner and meaner,'' Griff finished for him.

''Right,'' John growled.

''Well, Beast,'' Taylor said with a sardonic grin, ''that's just the way I want to keep you.''

When the two men entered his office James Morris felt fear. It was not the huge one that scared him most; it was the other one, the shorter (though not short) lean one with the dead eyes.

Griff Taylor.

"You're Taylor?" he asked, keeping his tone steady and firm.

"That's right."

"Who is that?"

"This is John."

"That's it?" Morris asked, puzzled not only by the man's name, but by his appearance, as well. "That's his name? Just John? No last name?"

"Some people call him John the Beast."

"The Beast?" Morris asked.

"He's my back-up."

Morris looked at the big man again and he could understand why "some people" had given him his nickname. He was certainly large enough — at least six-and-a-half feet tall — and incredibly wide, too. His hair was black and there was plenty of it — not only on his head, but on the backs of his hands, sticking out from the front of his shirt — probably all over his huge body.

The other man — easily six feet tall — wouldn't weigh more than one-sixty or so. He didn't look skinny, though; he looked wiry. He had dark hair, too, but his was thinner, coming to a widow's peak at his forehead. His eyes, though they looked dead, were active, darting all over the room; at the same time they always seemed to be looking at Morris. Morris found that disconcerting. He found everything about the man disconcerting. And yet he needed him.

He decided right then not to keep Griff Taylor around any longer than was absolutely necessary. Once the job was done, he'd pay him off and send him and his huge "back-up" on their way.

"Do you expect me to pay him?" Morris asked. "I hired you."

Taylor shrugged and said, ''It would be nice, but he doesn't necessarily care. He'll work for nothing.''

''He must be a good friend of yours to work for nothing,'' Morris observed.

''Friend?'' Griff Taylor didn't seem to understand the word. ''He's my back-up.'' That word made sense to him.

''Can we discuss why I'm here?'' Griff added, and to Morris it sounded more like a command than a question.

''All right,'' Morris said. ''Have a seat and we'll discuss it.''

''I prefer to stand,'' Taylor said. ''Start talking.''

That was when Morris realized this man would never allow him the upper hand in this — or any other — situation. He started talking.

CHAPTER SIXTEEN

"MAYBE WE SHOULD change our plans," said Andrew Carter when Liz had told him and Angie about her conversation with Morris.

"Our plans?" Angie asked.

"Yours and mine," Carter said, looking directly at his daughter. "Liz is leaving."

Angie looked at Liz, who said, "I still think it's best. Even if Morris tries to send his man after you, I don't think the man will do it."

"Why not?" Angie asked.

"It wouldn't be in keeping with his business," Liz explained. Liz herself hadn't actually known many gunmen—apart from Tate Gilmore, that is—and Tate's occupation had come as a surprise to her. When she first met Tate she thought he was just a travelling gunsmith. Then later — much later — she had found out that he was actually a gunman, or a "shootist," or any of the other terms that people used to describe men — people — who made their way with a gun.

Liz didn't make her living with a gun, but she did make her "way" with it, which she supposed made her eligible to be described in those same terms.

What she knew about gunmen she had learned from Tate. Now she passed on some of that knowledge to Angie.

"Gunmen are concerned with their reputations. They don't want people to think they're afraid; they don't want people to think that they won't do what they're paid to do; but they also don't want people to think they're —" she paused, groping for the word Tate had used, finding it, and using it, "— indiscriminate."

"Indi —"

"Crazy," Andrew Carter said for his daughter's benefit. "They don't want people to think that they'll kill just for the sake of killing."

"Right," Liz said. "Unless they *are* crazy."

"Is the man that Morris hired crazy?" Angie asked.

"We still don't know who he hired," Carter reminded her.

"Oh, that's right."

"And Liz can't afford to stay around to find out who it is," he added.

"It's not that I can't afford it," Liz protested. "I just think it's better for all of us if I leave."

"You're not afraid, are you?" Angie asked.

"Angie —"

"No, Andrew," Liz said, stopping him before he could scold her. "That's a fair question." Liz directed herself to Angie and said, "Yes, Angie, I am afraid, and I'd be a fool not to be." She had learned that, too, from Tate. "I'm afraid that I might get hurt, or killed, or that I might have to hurt or kill someone else.''

''I didn't think people like you —'' Angie began, and then stopped herself.

''Go ahead,'' Liz said. ''Finish what you were about to say.''

''I, uh —''

''You didn't think people like 'Angel Eyes' worried about that kind of thing,'' Liz said, completing Angie's thought for her.

Angie looked sheepish and nodded.

''People may have reputations, Angie, but they don't always deserve them.''

''You don't deserve yours?''

''Angie —'' Carter began, but once again Liz interrupted him.

''It's all right, Andrew,'' she said, placing a hand on his arm. ''She's curious. Angie, in a way I guess I do deserve it, at least to some extent. I've killed some men; but I don't think I've ever killed anyone without good reason.''

''People don't know that when they give you a reputation, do they?'' Angie asked.

''No, they don't.''

''I'm sorry.''

''That's all right.''

''You're not mad at me?''

''No, Angie, I'm not mad.''

''All right, now that that's settled,'' Carter said, ''can we get back to the business at hand?''

''She's across the street now,'' Morris said, looking out his window. He expected Taylor to walk over to the window and look, and when the man didn't he turned right around and said, pointing, ''Across the street, in the cafe.''

''That doesn't matter,'' Taylor said.

''Sure it does. She's right there; you can get the job done now.''

''That would mean rushing it.''

''So?'' Morris asked, not understanding.

''I never rush a job, Morris,'' Taylor said. ''I let them think about it for a while. It puts them at a disadvantage.''

''But she might leave town,'' Morris said. ''She might leave town today.''

''Have you spoken with her today?''

''Yes.''

''Did you tell her about me?''

''No. Yes. I mean —''

''What do you mean?''

''I told her that I had hired somebody, but I didn't tell her who.''

Aside from everything else that Morris found disconcerting about Griff Taylor, it also bothered him that the man seemed better educated than he had expected. The man who had given him Taylor's name had not told him anything about him except that he was fast, and good.

He hadn't said anything at all about him being an educated man, and oddly enough that bothered Morris.

''Then tell her,'' Taylor suggested — at least Morris wanted to believe it was a suggestion — ''and then she won't leave.''

''You think not?''

''Never mind,'' Griff Taylor said. ''I'll tell her. The cafe, you said?''

''That's right.''

''Beast.''

"Yeah?"

The huge man appeared totally uninterested in the proceedings. But now he looked at Griff Taylor, his great brow wrinkled with a sort of neanderthal — or perhaps infantile — concentration.

"Get us a couple of hotel rooms," Taylor instructed the big man. "I'll meet you at the hotel."

"Sure."

"And don't make any stops," Taylor added, wondering if the town had a whorehouse.

"Sure."

"Morris."

"Yes?"

"If you have any occasion to hire me again in the future," Taylor said, directing his cold, dead eyes into those of James Morris, "make damn sure you let me know beforehand who I'm facing."

"Why?" Morris asked. "I understood that you'd face anybody for money."

"This is a woman."

"So?"

"A woman costs more."

"I don't understand."

"I'm telling you that this will cost you more than you figured," Griff Taylor said, very slowly. Morris found that he resented the tone, because it resembled the one Taylor used when speaking to his back-up. "If that's a problem tell me now and I'll be on my way."

"Uh, no," Morris said quickly. "No, that won't be a problem. Uh, how much more?"

"If you have to ask," Taylor said, "it must be a problem."

"Uh, no, it's not. Really," Morris said. "It's no problem."

"Then I'll let you know," Taylor said, moving toward the door. "After."

Morris watched as Taylor walked through the door, and it soon became clear to him what "back-up" meant. The entire time Griff Taylor had his back turned, the large man — John — never took his eyes off Morris. Morris suspected that if he had made even the slightest wrong move, "the Beast" would have broken him in half.

After the huge man had followed Taylor out, disdainfully turning his own broad back on Morris, Morris's gaze swivelled back to the window to watch for them on the street.

When he realized he was sweating, he mopped his brow nervously.

CHAPTER SEVENTEEN

WHEN GRIFF TAYLOR stepped into the cafe, Liz knew who he was.

Oh, she didn't know who he was *by name*; but she knew that he was the man that James Morris had hired, and that he was looking for her.

"Andrew, why don't you take Angie and go back to the ranch?"

"Will we see you —?"

"I'll stop by before I make a final decision about leaving," she assured both of them.

Carter turned and saw the dark-clad stranger coming toward their table.

"Liz —"

"It's all right," she said. "He just wants to talk."

"How can you tell?" Carter murmured; but before she could answer the man had reached them.

"Liz Archer?"

"That's right."

"The one they call Angel Eyes?"

"Yes."

"Can we talk?"

"Sure."

The man looked at both of the Carters, and Andrew said, "We were just leaving." He and Angie stood up and he said to Liz, "See you at the ranch."

"Right."

Morris's gunman took the seat that Andrew Carter had just vacated and stared at Liz across the table. She noticed his eyes. Tate had always told her to watch a man's eyes, and watching this man's she knew that he had only come here to talk.

"So, talk," she said.

"I'm Griff Taylor."

She knew the name.

"So?"

"Do you know what I do?"

"Yes."

"Do you know why I'm here?"

"You said to talk," she said. "I have no reason to disbelieve you."

"No, I mean do you know why I'm here in Paragon?" the man asked again.

"I suppose I do. But instead of me guessing, why don't you just tell me?"

"All right," Taylor said. "I'm here to kill you."

"For money."

"Of course for money," Taylor said. "If you know my rep you know I don't kill for fun."

"Well, go back and tell Morris that I'm not going to co-operate."

"What's that mean?"

"That means that I'm leaving town."

"Really?"

"That's right. So there's no reason for you to stay around, either, because I won't face you."

"What makes you think I care whether you're facing me or not?"

"Your rep doesn't make you out to be a backshooter."

"So what? I've shot a few people in the back in my time. Just because you haven't heard that about me doesn't make it impossible."

"Are you telling me that if I don't face you you'll shoot me in the back?"

"Did I say that?"

"I don't like games, Mr. Taylor," Liz said, growing angry.

It surprised her, but she could see Griff Taylor responding to her as a woman.

"I don't think I've ever had such a pretty job to take care of."

"I'm flattered," Liz said. "I hadn't heard that you noticed such things, either, Mr. Taylor."

"Oh, I can appreciate beauty, Miss Archer. May I call you Elizabeth?"

"You can call me anything you like," Liz said, standing up. "I'm still leaving."

"I could make you stay, you know."

"How?"

"Your friends."

"They're . . . not my friends."

"Now who's playing games?"

Liz sat back down.

"Why would you want me to stay?"

"Let's just say I'm curious."

"About what?"

"About what it would be like."

"To kill a woman?"

Taylor shrugged.

"To draw on a woman, I guess."

"Don't you have more class than that, Taylor? Don't you have any regard for your rep?"

"I guess not."

She decided to try another tack.

"What would killing me do for your reputation, Taylor?"

"Call me Griff."

"Your rep is already far larger than mine. Killing me couldn't possibly add anything to it."

"A new experience."

"What?"

"It would be a new experience," Taylor repeated. "What's life without new experiences?"

It was amazing to her how the man could threaten her and flatter her with the same expression, in the same identical tone of voice.

"You wouldn't go after the Carters, would you?" she asked. She wondered idly if using her femininity on him would get her anywhere. She had seen him react to her, but almost immediately she rejected the idea as implausible. This kind of man would take her to bed, enjoy her — and probably make her enjoy him — and then calmly kill her.

"What do you think?"

"Goddammit, Taylor!" she said, standing up.

"Griff."

She glared at him, wishing she were a man—a man like Tate Gilmore — so she could beat him with her fists.

"I have someone with me, Elizabeth," he said then. "A man I call John the Beast. He's a huge man. Now, I have some little control over him most of the time, but not all of the time.''

''What are you telling me?''

''The daughter; what's her name? Angie?''

Liz didn't answer.

''It's Angie,'' Taylor said. ''She's kind of pretty. Not like you, but still pretty; and the Beast hasn't had a woman in a long time — and he needs to have women. You see, if he doesn't he just gets meaner and meaner, and soon I have no control over him at all. If he should see Angie Carter —''

''All right,'' Liz said, interrupting him. ''All right, Taylor. You win. Let's go out into the street and get it over with.''

Taylor stared at her, his face expressionless. Then he stood up and walked out.

Liz looked down at the table, picked up her coffee cup and sipped the cold, strong liquid. She steeled herself, got up and approached the door. She knew Griff Taylor's reputaton — Tate had told her about him. Taylor was good — he was real good — but even Tate admitted that he didn't know just *how* good.

She hoped that she would someday be able to tell him.

She stepped through the front door carefully, stopping just a couple of feet outside to look around. She couldn't see Taylor from there, so she stepped out further, to the end of the boardwalk.

Griff Taylor was nowhere in sight.

''You sonofabitch!'' she said in a low voice, from between her teeth.

She knew what he was doing. He was making her wait. All gunmen had their way of taking an edge, Tate had told her, and instinctively she knew that this was Taylor's way.

Well, she could take an edge, too.

All she had to do was figure out how.

"Looking for someone?"

Liz turned quickly in the direction of the voice. She was annoyed at herself. The speaker was Sheriff Bateman, and he should not have been able to get that close to her without her hearing him.

"No."

"Well, then, you won't be interested in the fact that Griff Taylor just went over to the hotel."

"Why should I be?"

"The way I see it, Miss Archer," Bateman said, "you and Taylor have an appointment."

"If we do I don't know when it is."

"I've seen enough of you people at work to know that he probably doesn't either," the lawman said. "But that doesn't make it any less of an appointment."

"What do you mean by 'you people?' " Liz asked.

"Oh, you know. Gunmen—although in your case I guess it's gunlady. What do you call yourself, anyway?"

"I never call myself," she said. She turned to walk away from him and spotted the smoke in the sky.

"Smoke," Bateman said.

"I see it," she said. "Can you tell where it's coming from?"

"I wouldn't swear to it," Bateman said speculatively, "but as a guess I'd say the Carter ranch."

"Oh, my God," Liz said, and started running toward the livery stable, with Bateman on her heels.

CHAPTER EIGHTEEN

WHEN THEY REACHED the Carter ranch the smoke was almost blindingly thick. The firefighters had formed a chain along which buckets of water passed from one willing pair of hands to the next. Liz could see Andrew and Angie Carter right in the thick of things, fighting the flames that threatened to engulf their barn.

"They need help," Bateman said, jumping down from his horse and rushing ahead of Liz. She leaped to the ground and followed.

They inserted themselves into the chain, lengthening it by two more links, and soon the fire's ferocity began to abate. Still, by the time the flames were quenched, a good half of the barn was gone.

"All right," Bateman said to Carter. "What happened?" Both men's faces were covered with black soot and their eyes stood out starkly against their black faces. Angie Carter came up next to her father and her face was the same. Liz wondered idly what she herself must look like.

"The fire was already going when we returned from town, Sheriff," Carter answered. "We'll have to find my foreman and ask him what happened."

"Are you all right?" Liz asked Angie.

"Yes, what about you?"

"I'm fine. We didn't get here until near the very end of the fire."

"No, I meant in town," Angie said. "How did everything go?"

"It didn't," Liz said, and when Angie frowned she added, "I'll explain later. Where's Ridge? Let's see what he can tell us about all this."

But when they found Ridge he could shed no light on how the fire might have started.

"We saw the flames and started fighting them right away," he explained. "We put out the flames on the roof of the house and then started on the barn."

"The house?" Angie exclaimed.

"It's fine," Ridge said. He was having some trouble breathing, as if he'd inhaled a lot of smoke, but he seemed to be handling it reasonably well and Liz didn't want to make a fuss. "We got to it right away."

"Thank God," Angie said.

"Ridge, you should have saved the barn," Carter said, scolding the man for what he considered poor judgement.

"Pa —"

"We had livestock in the barn," Carter explained. "We had supplies, feed. A lot of that is probably ruined, if not by the fire and smoke, then by the water. We could have rebuilt the house, Angie, but we can't replace what was in the barn — not without spending more money."

He left them at that point to go inside the barn and inspect the damage.

"Ridge —'' Angie said, putting her hand on the man's powerful arm.

He looked at her and said, "It's all right, Miss Angie. He's right, but —''

"But what?''

"I better go and check the livestock,'' he said. "We got them out of the barn in time.''

As the man walked away Angie stared at Liz and said, "I don't understand.''

"I think I do,'' Liz said.

"What?''

Sheriff Bateman had been staring at them and he chose that moment to head for the barn, following in Carter's wake. Liz moved closer to Angie.

"Let's get cleaned up.''

They walked to the water pump, brought up some clean water and washed as much black off their faces as possible.

"Liz, what —?''

"The house, Angie,'' Liz said. "That's where you live.''

"So?''

"So Ridge saved it for you,'' she explained. "He knew he should have saved the barn first, but he wanted to save the house for you.''

Angie looked about, as if searching for Ridge, but she couldn't find him. The hands were still milling about, putting out a few last stray flames.

"Liz, is he . . .?''

"What?'' Liz asked. "In love with you?''

Angie nodded and said, "Yes.''

"I think so.''

Hearing it confirmed seemed to shock Angie.

"He's older than me."

"That doesn't matter, Angie," Liz said. "You're not a child any more. You're a young woman."

"I wonder if Pa knows."

"I don't think so. I think it's something only a woman would see."

"I didn't."

"You've never been in love with a man and learned to read his feelings from the way he looks at you," Liz said. She was thinking about Chance Taker — or even about Tate Gilmore. She had not seen Tate in months, and before that had met up with him only twice, but she thought that he had feelings for her that he tried to deny. It was in his eyes when he looked at her.

"You have," Angie said, and Liz nodded.

"Yes," she said. "It's my guess that Ridge is very much in love with you, Angie."

"What do I do?" the younger woman asked in confusion.

"Nothing, right now," Liz answered. "There's too much going on to worry about it now. Let's go and see what the damage is in the barn, and then we can talk to your father and Sheriff Bateman. I wouldn't be surprised if Morris was behind this."

"Who else could it be?"

"No one else," Liz said. "I guess."

CHAPTER NINETEEN

THE LAST THING Liz Archer expected was that she would find herself in bed with Sheriff Pete Bateman later that day, after they returned from the Carter ranch together. Perhaps it was the fact that they had fought the fire together, or maybe it was just that they were attracted to one another.

Perhaps she really was over Chance, at least enough to start living again, to start being interested in other men.

While Bateman busied himself between her legs, using his tongue to tease her straining clit, she tried to prolong the moment by thinking back to how it had come about . . .

They had ridden back to town together, after Liz had discussed the situation with the Carters.

"I think you'd best keep Angie here now, Andrew," she said. "With Ridge watching her, as you orginally planned."

"Why can't I go with you?" Angie asked.

"Because I've got Griff Taylor hanging over my head," Liz explained. "And I don't need you hanging around my neck. I'm not trying to be cruel —"

"I understand. But what happened to your plan to leave town?"

Liz shrugged and said, "Plans change."

At that point Bateman came over and announced he was returning to town.

"We appreciate your help, Sheriff," Carter said, although the fact that he really didn't like Bateman was written all over his face.

"It's my job, Carter," Bateman replied. "That's all."

"Do you mind if I ride back with you?" Liz asked.

"Not at all."

When they reached town and after they had put their horses up at the livery Liz said, "I badly need a bath."

"So do I. You might as well go over to the hotel and take yours. I have to go to my office, and you should be done by the time I get back to the hotel."

"You bathe at the hotel?"

"They have the best facilities," Bateman explained. "And, yes, I do bathe on occasion."

"That's not what I meant."

"No," Bateman said, studying her, "it probably isn't. I'm sorry."

"That's all right."

"Maybe we should talk again . . . later," he suggested, and Liz nodded. Neither of them guessed then what form their conversation would take.

It had to have been an accident, she decided afterward. She didn't think Bateman had planned it the way it happened.

Or maybe it was the desk clerk's idea of a joke . . .

She had just stepped dripping from her bath and reached for a towel, when the door opened and Bateman walked in.

"Oh!" he said, stopping short and staring in frank admiration at her magnificent body. Her flesh glistened from the water, which dripped off the tips of her large breasts, drop by drop from her rigid nipples . . .

"I'm sorry," he stammered, unable to stop staring. The triangle of pale hair between her legs was darkened by the water.

"Are you?" she asked. It was a snap decision on her part not to grope for a towel to cover herself. Oddly, she felt herself becoming aroused. The sheriff was not bad looking, and he was in excellent shape himself. He had been removing his shirt as he entered, and she could see that his hairy chest was solid, as was his belly.

"You don't think I planned this, do you?" he asked, indignantly.

"Didn't you?"

"I did not," he said. "The clerk told me the room was empty."

"I see."

They stood for several seconds, staring at each other.

"You don't believe me."

"It doesn't matter."

"Yes, it does," he said, closing the door behind him. The chilly draft had made her nipples even harder.

He moved toward her and said, "If I had wanted to make advances to you, I could have thought of a better way, believe me."

"Oh, I do."

She reached casually for the towel, the movement causing her breasts to grow taut. She saw his eyes follow her, and as he licked his lips she knew he was going to do something.

"By God, woman," he said huskily, and stepped forward to take her into his arms.

Not surprised, she went willingly, pressing her damp body against him, feeling the coarse hair on his chest against her distended nipples.

The first time was right there on the floor, an incredibly sensual and memorable experience.

Shucking his clothes, he bore her to the floor with him, so they lay naked together with not even a towel beneath them to protect them from the wooden floorboards. Idly, Liz wondered if she would pick up splinters in her buttocks.

His penis was swollen, long and slim, and she wrapped her hands around it, teasing the spongy head with her thumbs.

When he kissed her he thrust his tongue deeply into her mouth and she sucked on it avidly. His hands began to rove over her body eagerly, finally settling between her legs. He delved into her moistness with first one finger, then another, while flicking her clit with his thumb.

"Mmm." She moaned into his mouth, urging him on, though he needed little urging. He mounted her, poked her portal with the head of his erection, and then plunged into her forcefully, bringing a gasp from her mouth into his.

He rode her hard, driving deeply into her with repeated thrusts, and she wrapped her legs around his hips tightly, oblivious to the bruises on her smooth buttocks from the hardwood floor . . .

Now, as his tongue urged her on to another orgasm, she grasped the back of his head and began to move her hips in unison with the thrusts of his tongue and his lips. He slid his hands beneath her to cup her buttocks and control her tempo. She was completely at his mercy and not disliking it a bit . . .

Finally, when her body shook uncontrollably with completion, he wasted no time in mounting her again and plunging into her. The mattress gave beneath her as he drove into her. The floor had actually allowed him better penetration, but she was not about to stop him to suggest they move to the floor.

Both of them were way beyond stopping, or wanting to . . .

"That was incredible."

"Which?" she asked. "The sex, or that we had sex?"

"Both," he said. They were lying side by side in her bed at the hotel, staring at the ceiling. "I really didn't plan this, you know."

"I believe you."

"You keep saying that."

"I do believe you."

"I wish I had, though."

"What?"

"Planned this," he said. "It would have been a damn good idea."

"Pete —"

"What?"

"Shut up," she said, rolling against him . . .

She licked his nipples, enjoying the way they hardened beneath her tongue, then licked her way down over his belly to where his penis stood at attention, jutting out from the dense tangle of his pubic hair. She rubbed his erection along one cheek and then the other, then opened her mouth and allowed the swollen head to slide past her lips.

"Oh, God," he moaned as she took more of him into her mouth while cupping his sack gently.

"Mmmm," she replied, avidly sucking on him. He raised his hips off the bed in response to the suction of her mouth, and then she felt his testicles tighten and his penis swell, before he started to ejaculate forcefully . . .

"That wasn't such a bad idea, either," he said, moments later.

"No, it wasn't." She held his flaccid penis in her hand, using her thumb to play with the little slit on the top.

"Now that we're on such good speaking terms, though," he began.

"Yes?"

"There is something that is a bad idea."

"What?"

"Your staying in town."

She propped herself up on one elbow so she could look down at him. "You're telling me to leave town?"

"Asking."

"Why?"

"Why?" he repeated. "I would think that's obvious."

"Griff Taylor?"

"Of course," Bateman said. "We know he's working for Morris, and what else is he here for if not to kill you?"

"Or to try."

"You're a tough lady," he said. "I admit that, okay?"

"I'm not tough," she argued. "I just know what I have to do."

"Which is?"

"I've got to stay, Pete, or Taylor and his friend will go after the Carters — both of them."

"Andrew mean that much to you?'' he asked, trying to make it sound casual.

"Angie, too,'' she said, which didn't really answer his question. "I don't want Taylor going after them because he can't get me.''

"So he'll kill you, and then go after them, anyway,'' Bateman said.

"Oh? You've got him killing me, already?''

"Aw, come on, Liz,'' he said. "I know you have a reputation, but it's nothing like his.''

"Which naturally means that I won't have a chance, right?''

He moved up onto his elbow so that their faces were scant inches apart.

"I don't want to fight with you,'' he said. "I don't know if he's faster than you or not, but I'm afraid to find out. I may have to go and talk to him, myself.''

"Pete,'' she said, shaking her head, "how fast are you with a gun?''

"Not very,'' he admitted. "But that's beside the point. This is my town. I'm the law.''

"That gives you an edge?''

"It should.''

"It should,'' she said. "But it won't. Not against the likes of Griff Taylor and his . . . his beast.''

"Beast?''

She explained to him what Taylor had told her about his companion.

"Well, it doesn't matter to me how many of them there are,'' he said. "If you won't leave town, I'll have to tell them to.''

He started to get out of bed, but she held fast to his penis, which rose beneath the pressure of her hand.

"You're a brave man, right?"

"I'm a lawman."

"Then how about upholding one of my laws?"

"Which is?"

She squeezed his penis and said, "Never leave a lady half satisfied."

"Half—?" he stammered, then saw her grin and knew that she was teasing.

She was more than half satisfied . . . but she was far from finished.

CHAPTER TWENTY

JAMES MORRIS was livid.

The objects of his anger were his men, Tracy and Lon. It seemed that Tracy had gotten tired of watching and waiting and had decided to take some action of his own.

Like starting a fire.

"It was Tracy's idea," mush-mouthed Lon insisted when he and Tracy entered Morris's office.

"Get lost, Lon," Morris said, and Lon left.

"Tracy —"

"Look, I just thought it was time we did something to get them out," Tracy insisted. "We didn't even have to leave the Archer woman alone for long. In fact, I left Lon to watch her."

"That's just fine," Morris said. "So you're making the decisions now, is that it?"

"Boss, I just thought —"

"Damn you, Tracy, you *didn't* think. That's the trouble with you, you never think. You don't have the capacity to think, you moron!"

"You don't have to —"

"Who's going to be the first one the sheriff comes looking for about this?"

"I don't —"

"Me, you idiot! Not even you. It'll be me he comes after."

"I didn't —"

"You didn't think. Right?"

Tracy remained silent, wishing he had the guts to reach across and slap Morris in the face. Still, Morris had the money and the power, and Tracy wanted a share of that, so he withstood Morris's anger silently.

"How much damage was done?"

"I'm not sure," Tracy said. "I think the barn was burned pretty bad."

"And the house?"

"They got to that pretty quick."

"What about damage to livestock?"

"None," Tracy said. "They got them out of the barn in time."

"You didn't accomplish very much with your fire, did you, Tracy?"

"I suppose not."

"Are you ready to go back to doing what you're told?" Morris demanded.

"Yes."

"Then keep an eye on Liz Archer."

"Yes, sir."

"Where is she now?"

"Over at the hotel."

"Where's the sheriff?"

"Over at the hotel."

"Are they together?"

"I don't know."

Bateman, Morris thought viciously. What would he know about satisfying a woman like that? Just once, he thought, he'd like to get her into his bed, just once before Griff Taylor killed her.

"Boss?"

"What?"

"Should I go now?"

"God, yes. Get out of my sight."

Tracy backed away, then turned and hurried through the door.

Morris sat back in his chair and stared into space, smoothing his hair.

Just once . . .

"Now where are you going?" Liz asked as Bateman sat up in bed.

"Don't tell me you're still not satisfied," he said, staring at her in mock disbelief.

"You did very well by the lady, thank you very much, sir," she said humbly.

"Well, you didn't do so bad yourself," he said, leaning over and kissing her. Then he stood up and began to dress.

"So?"

"So what?" he said.

"Where are you going?"

"I've got a fire to look into."

"Where will you start?"

"Where else?"

"With Morris?"

"Right. Who else would have a motive to burn the Carters out?"

"I'm coming," she said, swinging her feet off the bed and planting them on the floor.

"No," he said. "You're not."

"Why not?"

"Because you're not a deputy, and because I don't want you anywhere near Morris."

"What do you expect me to do, then?"

"I don't suppose you'd wait right here?"

"Only if you wait with me."

"I didn't think so. You intend to walk around and make yourself a target for Griff Taylor?"

"I'm already a target," she said. "He'll come after me when he's ready. Unless . . ."

"Unless what?" he asked, looking at her suspiciously.

"Unless I force him to face me before he's ready," she said, more to herself than to him. "Before he's got the edge he thinks he needs. Maybe that would be *my* edge."

"Your edge," Bateman said, "would be me behind Taylor with a shotgun."

"Oh, no," she said, bounding off the bed so violently that her breasts swayed and slapped each other audibly. "When the time comes, Peter, you've got to promise me you won't interfere."

"I'm the law," he said, pompously. "If I want to interfere —"

"It'll be a fair fight," she assured him. "Taylor's rep won't let him do it any other way."

"What about the other one?"

"You can keep an eye on him, if you like," she said. "But leave Taylor be."

"Liz —"

"Promise?"

"I can't."

"You've got to."

"I promise I'll try to stay out of it," he said. "But you're not just Angel Eyes to me any more, Liz. I may not be able to stand by while —"

She put her arms around his neck and pressed her warm body against his, kissing him with equal warmth.

"You're a dear man."

"Uh-huh," he said skeptically.

"Go ahead and have your talk with Morris. Will you let me know what he says?"

"Sure, over dinner."

"Okay."

She kissed him again, briefly, and then he left.

Idly she examined herself in the mirror, preening. She was satisfied with herself, with the way she'd handled herself with Andrew Carter and Pete Bateman. She had enjoyed them as friends, and she hoped that they would feel that way about her, too. She still was not ready to commit emotionally to a man, but she was beyond the point where she would avoid contact with them altogether.

Rubbing her hands over her smooth, firm buttocks, counting the bruises from the hardwood floor, she was glad to be at that *point* in her life — although it could have come at a better *time*.

CHAPTER TWENTY-ONE

FROM JOHN THE BEAST'S hotel room Griff Taylor had been able to observe the smoke and guess where it was probably coming from.

"How does it look?" John asked from his position on his bed.

"Under control," Taylor said. "The smoke is starting to fade away."

"Guess they put it out, then. Do you still think it's that ranch?"

"Yes."

"How does that affect the job?"

"It doesn't," Taylor said. "The Carters are Morris's problem. Mine is Angel Eyes."

"I heard of her," John said. "Is she as pretty as I heard?"

"Prettier."

"Damn."

Taylor looked over at the bed then and saw the reason for John's curse. The front of the big man's pants was straining to hold his massive erection. Taylor knew that he himself had an impressive penis, but he'd had occasion once or twice to see the big man naked and was always amazed at the size of his member. He wondered how any woman could possibly accommodate its full length.

"Whaddaya think of this fella Morris?"

"Not much," Taylor admitted, examining the street. "He's probably got this town under his thumb, but that don't mean he's much. He's having trouble with a rancher and his daughter."

"He ought to just kill 'em."

"He won't," Taylor said. "But he might want us to."

"Will we?"

"I haven't decided."

"I don't know how much longer I can hold out, Griff," John the Beast said, grabbing his crotch, attempting to adjust himself so as to be less uncomfortable.

"You'll hold out as long as you have to, John," Taylor assured him.

"I'm gonna have to break somebody in half, then."

"You might get that opportunity," Taylor said as he watched the sheriff leave the hotel and cross the street toward James Morris's office. "You just might get that chance."

"You like fires, Morris?" Bateman asked. He entered the man's office without knocking and found him seated at his desk.

"What are you talking about?"

"I'm talking about fire."

"I think you've got a touch of the sun, Bateman," Morris said.

"You don't know anything about a fire out at the Carter ranch, is that right?"

"Yes, that's right. I had nothing to do with it."

"I find that real hard to believe, Morris," Bateman said. "There's nobody else in this town with a motive to burn those people out."

"I say there is," Morris said, "because it wasn't me who did it."

"Then it was your men."

"Talk to them, then," Morris said, "and leave me alone. I have some business to take care of."

"So do I, Morris," Bateman said. "And you're at the top of my list. Remember that."

James Morris studied the lawman for a few moments and then said, "I haven't forgotten about that town council meeting, you know. You won't be wearing that badge for very much longer, Bateman."

"As long as I am wearing it," Bateman said, "I'll continue to do my job. I'll find out who set that fire, Morris. Count on it."

"Get out of my office."

Bateman walked to the door, opened it, and then turned back to say one last thing.

"I'm warning you, Morris, man to man," he said. "Badge or no badge. No harm better come to Liz Archer, or I'm coming after you."

After Bateman left, Morris turned to face the window, biting his lip and frowning. Things were getting out of hand. They had been going that way ever since Liz Archer arrived in Paragon. All he needed now was Bateman on his back for the rest of the sheriff's term. In spite of what he had told the lawman, he didn't think he'd be able to get the town council to kick him out of the job.

With Griff Taylor in town, Elizabeth Archer was as good

as dead. Bateman had obviously become friendly with her — although what she saw in the man escaped Morris completely — and when Taylor did kill her, the lawman would come after him for sure.

He wondered how much extra Taylor would charge for a sheriff.

All of a sudden it struck Liz that there was only one hotel in Paragon.

She got dressed and went downstairs to talk to the desk clerk, who could not seem to break the habit of staring at her.

"I'd like to see the register, please."

"Uh, are you worried that you didn't check in?" he asked nervously.

"No, I know I checked in," she said, patiently. "I'd just like to see the register, please."

"Is there something I can help you with?" the clerk asked eagerly. Liz decided she had probably wronged him in thinking that he might have deliberately sent Bateman walking in on her during her bath.

"I'm interested in finding out if someone is registered in the hotel."

"Who?"

"A tall, slender man dressed in dark clothes," she said. And when that didn't seem to prod his memory she added, "With a gorilla who should be on a leash."

"Oh, them," the clerk said. "Yes, they registered just today."

"Is there another place to stay in town?"

"You don't like your room?" he asked. "I can change it if you like."

"No, the room's fine," she said. "I'm just interested in knowing if there is another place in town."

"Well, there's a rooming house at the south end of town . . . but it's not as nice —"

"Don't worry," she said. "Thank you for the information."

"Sure. Anything I can do to help."

She went back to her room, feeling silly for her momentary thought of moving to the rooming house. Why should she? In fact, why should she wait for Taylor to make the first move? Perhaps, as she had thought earlier, her edge *was* to force him into a confrontation before he was ready.

Liz Archer was still not long out of her girlhood. She'd had to grow up into Angel Eyes very quickly. She had not been at it long enough to be able to isolate her "edge." It would take time before she was sure enough of it to move; but soon she would.

She only hoped that soon was early enough.

Tate Gilmore, with all your instincts and knowledge — where are you when I need you?

CHAPTER TWENTY-TWO

AFTER SEEING MORRIS, Sheriff Bateman went to his office, but he only stayed there for half an hour. It took him that long to decide to go and see Griff Taylor.

"What room is Taylor in?" he asked the clerk.

"Taylor," the clerk said, starting to look at the register.

"The man with the big friend."

"Oh, him," the clerk said, closing the book. "He's in fourteen, and his friend is in four."

"Overlooking the street?"

"Yes."

As Bateman started for the steps the clerk said, "She was asking about them, too."

"Who?"

"The lady."

"Liz Archer?"

"Yes."

"Did she go to see him?" Bateman asked anxiously.

"I don't think so."

"Thanks."

Bateman went up the steps, started for room fourteen, and then changed his mind and headed for room four. It wasn't Taylor's room, but it was the one that overlooked the street.

That's where a gunman would be, although it wouldn't be where he'd want to sleep.

When John the Beast opened his door he looked down at the face of the man, and then at the badge.

"Law," he said aloud.

"Let him in."

The big man backed away and allowed Sheriff Bateman to enter.

"Taylor?" Bateman said.

Taylor, standing by the window, said, "That's right," without looking behind him. "What can I do for the law, Sheriff?"

"You could leave town."

"Sorry."

"Barring that, you could forget about working for James Morris."

"Who?"

"Morris," the sheriff repeated. "And while you're at it, you could also forget about Liz Archer."

"Am I supposed to know what you're talking about?" Taylor asked.

"You do."

After a pause Taylor said, "If I *were* working for some-one, and you wanted me to stop, would you be willing to match what he was paying me?"

"Willing, maybe," Bateman said. "But not able."

"Then we'd have nothing to talk about, would we, Sheriff?"

"Oh, yes," Bateman said. "We would, and we do."

Taylor finally turned away from the window to look at the sheriff, who noticed the dark, flat, emotionless eyes of the gunman.

A killer's eyes.

"This is your town, Sheriff," Taylor said, "so I'm being courteous."

"I appreciate it."

"I'm sure you do, but I've about reached the limit of that courtesy. We are in my associate's room, and I think he wants you to leave."

"That's fine with me," Bateman said. He did not even glance at the huge man standing off to his right. "We'll talk again, when you're in your own room."

"Fine."

"About Liz Archer," the lawman said, moving toward the door. "About how anyone who wants to do her harm will have to come through me."

As Bateman left, Taylor said to John, "Do you know what you call a man who's willing to die for a woman?"

"What?"

Taylor turned back to the window and said, "A fool."

CHAPTER TWENTY-THREE

TWO DAYS PASSED without incident, and several people began to get edgy.

First was Morris himself.

How long, he wondered, was Griff Taylor going to wait? He spent most of his day staring out his window at the hotel across the street. Goddamn, he thought, they're even in the same hotel together. Until Griff Taylor decided to move Morris could make no progress toward taking over Andrew Carter's ranch. Angel Eyes had to be out of the way first.

Damn it, Taylor, what are you waiting for?

Tracy and Lon were getting edgy, too.

Well, Tracy was getting edgy; Lon was getting nervous. It had become obvious to them both that Liz Archer knew they were watching her. Lon was worried she'd decide to try and kill them.

Tracy was worried that she wouldn't.

Andrew Carter was trying to go about his work, but in the back of his mind he wondered when Morris would make another try at the ranch, or at Angie?

And what was happening between Griff Taylor and Liz Archer?

Angie wondered about Liz. Was she even still in town? Yes, of course she was. She had said that she wouldn't leave until her business with Morris's gunman was finished.

And when that time came, would she be able to leave? Would she still be alive?

"Pa, I'm worried."

"About the ranch?"

"About Liz."

"Yes," he admitted. "So am I."

"She might die because she wanted to help us."

"I know."

"Can't we do something?"

"We're doing what we can," Carter said, "to save our ranch."

"And Liz?"

"She can take care of herself," Carter reminded his daughter. "Isn't she called Angel Eyes?"

"That doesn't mean that she'll be able to stand up to this Griff Taylor," Angie said.

Carter took his daughter by the shoulders and told her the truth.

"Angie, we know that *we* can't stand up to a man like

Griffin Taylor,'' he said. ''Whether or not Angel Eyes
can remains to be seen.''

"Then we just wait?''

"Yes,'' he said, ''we protect ourselves, our land and
our home — and we wait.''

Ridge was edgy, and it had nothing to do with Liz Archer,
James Morris or Griff Taylor.

Angie Carter was the only thing on his mind.

"What's he waiting for?'' Bateman asked.

Liz snuggled closer to the lawman, kissed his chest and
said, ''He's trying to get his edge.''

"Which is?''

"To make me nervous.''

"And are you?''

"Of course.''

"Scared?''

"That, too.''

"What are you going to do about it?''

"I've just about got that figured.''

"And?''

"And I think I've finally figured out — *my* edge,'' she
said, moving her hand beneath the sheet.

He wanted to ask her to explain, but suddenly her head
followed her hand and her tongue began to bring his penis
ragingly erect.

She took it in her mouth when it was impossibly swollen
and sucked it avidly, holding it with one hand around the
base, and the other caressing his balls.

Jesus, he thought, he'd never known a woman like her.
She wore a gun and, according to reputation, used it better
than most men, and yet when she was in bed with him —

or with any other man, no doubt — she was all woman.

With a great groan he came in her mouth and she accommodated his emission without difficulty. Even after his spasms had stopped, she continued to work on him with her tongue, her teeth, her lips, her breasts; and then while she held him there in the valley between those incredible mounds of smooth, pale flesh, he felt himself swelling again — larger, if possible, than before.

She came from beneath the sheet and laid her body atop him, her breast smashed against his chest, her pelvis thrusting into his. He moved his hands to her buttocks, gripped them tightly, and entered her . . .

As Pete Bateman speared her she felt her breath catch in her throat. She wanted this to be the best she'd ever had, because tomorrow would be the day she'd face Griff Taylor.

Whether he was ready or not.

CHAPTER TWENTY-FOUR

THE NEXT DAY did not go quite as Angel Eyes had planned.

In the morning when she awoke next to Pete Bateman they had an argument

No, they had a fight.

Bateman insisted that she leave Paragon, saying that he had a "feeling" that Griff Taylor wouldn't wait much longer.

"He won't be able to," she said coolly, starting to dress.

"Why do you say that?"

"Because I'm not waiting for him."

"What?"

"I'm calling him out today."

"You're crazy."

"No," she said. "I was crazy not to do it two days ago, but I admit that I was scared. Now, I'm ready."

"And so is he."

"Maybe not," she said. "We'll see."

She stood up and strapped on her gun, and Bateman hurriedly climbed into his pants and began to struggle with his boots.

"Wait for me."

"Stay out of it, Pete."

"I'm the law, damn it," he said, dropping his left boot in his haste.

"I'll see you later, Pete."

As she headed for the door Bateman began to shout, but she ignored him.

She went to room fourteen and pounded on the door.

"Rise and shine, Taylor," she called out loudly. "It's time."

There was no answer. She pounded again for quite a while, but still there was no answer.

"Sonofabitch."

She hurried down the hall to room four and repeated her pounding, with the same result.

She went downstairs and found the clerk behind the desk.

"Rooms fourteen and four," she said. "Did the men go out?"

"Go out?" he asked, frowning. "Ma'am, they checked out."

"When?"

"Early this morning."

"Early?" she asked. It was eight now. They must have checked out at first light.

"That sonofabitch," she said again.

"Excuse me?" the clerk said.

She was angry at first, and then she felt a hint of fear.

However, by the time Pete Bateman came stomping down the steps, she was actually smiling.

"What happened?" he demanded, puzzled.

"He's checked out."

"Taylor?"

"Yes."

Looking satisfied, Bateman said, "Good. Then it's over, for whatever reason —"

"Oh, it's not over, Pete," she said.

"But he's gone?"

"He's only checked out of the hotel."

"So?"

"So he still has the edge," she said. "I waited too long to make up my mind."

"I don't understand?"

"Why would he check out?"

"Because he was leaving town."

"And he's not going to leave town until he's done his job — or tried to."

"So he's leaving today —"

"— after we've had our . . . meeting." She folded her arms beneath her breasts and said, "*He's* picked today, not me. I'm totally without an edge."

"You sound like you admire him."

"I suppose I do," she admitted. "He's out-thought me at every turn. I think he even figured out how long it would take me to make up my mind."

"So now what happens?"

"I'll have to wait," she replied. "He'll show himself today, when he's ready."

"You could still leave."

'No, I can't. I'm curious."

"Curious? About what?"

She looked at him and said, "I'm really starting to wonder how it will turn out."

He looked at her as if he were seeing her for the first time.

"You're after a reputation."

She started and stared at him.

"I am not!"

"Yes, Liz, you are," he said. "That's what is making you stay; that's what is making you face Griffin Taylor, the gunman, the man with the reputation."

She waited a moment before speaking, thinking his words over and mixing them with words spoken by Tate Gilmore.

Tate had a rep, and although he was not ashamed of it, he was not proud of it, either. It was there, he said, like his eyes, like his *breath* — and without his breath how long would he last?

Did she want that kind of life?

"No," she said, "you are wrong, Pete. This is simply something that I must do, and I think I'm allowed to be curious about the outcome."

He stared at her as she turned and left the hotel lobby.

Griff Taylor was out there somewhere and she knew that the time of their meeting would be of his choosing. But she'd be damned if she was going to sit and wait and be easy for him to find.

She left the hotel, saddled Blossom and rode toward the Carter ranch.

"Pa!" Angie called, rushing to the corral where her father was schooling a difficult colt. He was hoping the animal would set the tone for the prices he'd get from the army for the rest of the horses.

"Angie, I'm trying —"

"Liz is here."

"Is she all right?"

"She looks fine," Angie said happily. "Come inside and have coffee with us."

Carter wrestled with himself. He wanted to see Liz, but he had to finish off this colt.

"I'll be in in a few minutes, honey. Tell her to wait for me."

"All right," she said, shaking her head. "I'll tell her, Pa."

Angie rushed back to the house, where she had left Liz sitting over a cup of coffee.

"He has to finish what he's doing, but he'll be in real soon. I know he's anxious to see you."

"I told you not to bother him while he was working."

"It's no bother."

Angie got herself a cup of coffee and sat opposite Liz.

"What happened?"

"What do you mean?"

"With Morris's gunman, Griff Taylor," Angie said, leaning forward eagerly. "Is it over?"

"It hasn't begun."

Angie frowned and said, "I don't understand."

"He outfoxed me," Liz said readily, and explained to Angie how.

"And you're not angry?"

"I was," Liz said. "And I was afraid."

"And now?"

"Now I'm waiting for him to pick his time."

Carter entered the house just in time to hear this.

"That's crazy!"

"You're the second man to tell me that today," Liz said,

looking at him. "And you're wrong, too, Andrew."

"Liz —"

"I worked it out on the way here, Andrew," she interrupted him. "I'm willing to face him whenever and wherever he chooses."

"Crazy," Carter said again, but Liz didn't even hear him.

"Don't you see?" she asked. "That's it, that's just what I've been waiting to find."

"I don't understand," Angie said.

Liz looked at her and said, "I've finally found it, Angie. The willingness to face him on his terms." She paused, unintentionally giving her statement dramatic effect, and then said, "That's my edge!"

CHAPTER TWENTY-FIVE

"WHAT?!"

James Morris was aghast at the news Jack Tracy had just imparted to him.

"Lon is following the woman, but Taylor and his man have checked out of the hotel. In fact, they checked out at first light."

"He can't do that!"

"Really?" Tracy said. "Well, you find him and tell him that."

"Watch you mouth, Tracy," Morris said. "Just because you've never seen me get physical doesn't mean I can't."

Morris kept himself in good condition, but the burly Tracy had no doubt that he could handle the man if he did indeed try to "get physical."

He hoped it wouldn't come to that, though.

Not yet, anyway.

"What should we do?" he asked.

Morris rubbed his thumbnail over his lower lip in an agitated gesture, then said, "All right."

"What?"

"It's time we took care of Andrew Carter."

"Kill him?"

"No," Morris said. "The girl. Grab his daughter, Angie."

"And do what with her?"

"Bring her to the house."

"To your place?"

Morris pinned Tracy with a hard stare and said, "To Sarah's."

Same thing, Tracy thought.

"All right."

"Once we have his daughter," Morris said, "we'll have his ranch."

"You'll have *her*."

As Tracy turned and walked toward the door Morris called out, "Don't mess it up this time, Tracy."

Tracy turned and said, "Angel Eyes?"

"Take more men," Morris said. "I'll pay them. Take more men and if she gets in the way, you kill her, Tracy. You hear me? Kill her."

Tracy's heart began to beat faster and he said, "Yes, sir."

Tracy found Lon in the place they usually watched the Carter ranch from. Tracy had three other men with him.

"Why all the men?"

"We're making a move."

"Finally!" Lon said. "What's the plan?"

"We're taking the girl."

"Angel Eyes?"

Tracy shook his head.

"The daughter. Angie."

"What about the other one?"

"Her we're going to kill," Jack Tracy said, with relish.

Sheriff Pete Bateman got over his anger and went looking for Liz Archer. When he couldn't find her — or Morris's men, Tracy and Lon — he went straight to Morris's office.

"You're too late, "Morris told the lawman as he came bursting into his office.

"What do you mean?"

Morris had already decided to tell Bateman the truth, because he knew that would send the lawman out to the Carter ranch to try and save Liz Archer.

He hoped neither of them would come back alive.

"It's going to come to an end out at the Carter ranch," Morris said.

"What have you done?"

"I've decided to stop beating around the bush, Sheriff," Morris said, leaning forward. "I've decided to go ahead and take what I want."

Bateman's heart began to beat faster. If that were the case, then Morris would have sent more than just Tracy and Lon. Those two Liz could handle. But how many others . . .?

"I'll be back for you, Morris," Bateman said. "That's a promise."

"One you won't keep," Morris replied. But Bateman was not there to hear him.

Morris rose and decided to go to the house and wait with Sarah. It was about to happen. Looking at the map on the wall he knew that he was about to gain that little piece of land that would complete his uncompleted puzzle. He was the most powerful man in the county, and his power would spread — as the feeling of power was now spreading through his loins.

He had the largest erection he'd ever had, and he needed Sarah Medford now more than ever. As powerful as the sensation was now, he knew the feeling would be even more tremendous once he was between her legs.

CHAPTER TWENTY-SIX

"WHERE'S RIDGE?" Liz asked.

"He's supervising the repairs on the barn," Carter said. "Why?"

"I think maybe we should get together and work out a plan, in case —"

"The only plan that I can see is for you to stay here," Carter interrupted her. "If Morris's gunman wants you, let him come here."

"No, that won't work," Liz said.

"I'll get Ridge," Angie said.

Carter looked at her, said, "All right," and went back to arguing with Liz.

Angie left the house in search of Ridge. She had volunteered so that she could talk to him alone, first. She thought that maybe it was time for them to talk.

She knew that the rear of the barn had been gutted and

that a whole new wall had to be built, so she started around the far side of the barn to get there.

That was a mistake, because it took her out of sight of the house . . .

"All right," Tracy said. "Let's move in closer."

"Me?" Lon said.

"No, you stay here and cover us," Tracy ordered. He looked at one of the other men and said, "You come with me."

He'd picked out three men who were regulars around town. He knew their faces, though he couldn't remember their names. They were all working along for a quick hundred dollars, and none of them particularly cared what they had to do to earn it.

"Let's go," he said to the man, and they started toward the house.

They were just approaching the barn when Tracy saw Angie Carter coming around the corner of the building, into their view, and out of sight of the house.

"Well, well," he said. "Who could have guessed it would be this easy?"

Liz and Andrew's "discussion" was interrupted by the sound of a volley of shots.

"Jesus—" Carter said, immediately thinking of Angie.

They both jumped up — Carter grabbing a rifle from a rack on the wall — and ran out of the house. It was Liz who pinpointed the location of the shots.

"Around the barn!"

They ran together toward the barn, then split up, taking opposite routes around the building.

As Liz rounded her corner she saw Ridge firing his gun and ran up to him.

"What happened?" she demanded. All she could see in the direction he'd been firing were clouds of dust.

Carter came up on them from the other direction. "Where's Angie?" he said frantically. "She came out here to get you."

Ridge looked at his boss and said, "They took her."

"What? How?"

Ridge answered, looking sick.

"She was coming around this side of the barn, so none of us saw her until it was too late. We heard her shout, and as we came around someone started firing at us."

He inclined his head toward the body of one of the hands. The man lay in the dust, riddled with bullet holes. Ridge's left shoulder was bloody where a bullet had creased him.

"Who was it?" Carter demanded.

"Tracy."

"Damn!" Carter swore, and turned impulsively toward the barn.

"Andrew, wait!" Liz called.

"For what?" the man demanded. "Morris has my daughter now. He can have my land as long as he gives her back."

"That's what he wants!"

"Then that's what he'll get!" Carter shouted. 'I was a fool to think I could beat him."

"Wait, damn it!" she shouted again.

"Liz —"

"Let's find out what we're up against before we go off half-cocked."

"We?"

"I'm not about to let you go after her alone."

"Neither am I," Ridge said.

Liz turned her attention to the foreman and said, "How many men were there?"

"I counted four or five," Ridge answered, "but there

could have been more. Two of them — Tracy and another — grabbed her, and we were fired on from that clump of brush out there. There must have been at least five."

"That means that Tracy and Lon have help now."

"Taylor?" Carter asked.

"Not likely," Liz said. "He's got his own job to do, and I think what happened is that his move this morning fooled Morris."

"What do you mean?"

"I mean that when Taylor checked out of the hotel Morris thought he was backing out of his job and overreacted."

"By grabbing Angie."

"Right."

At that moment, the sound of approaching hoofbeats arrested their attention.

"They're coming back," Carter cried out, raising his rifle.

"Hold on," Liz snapped, knocking the barrel of Carter's rifle down. "It's the sheriff."

She recognized Bateman before anyone else, but of course there was good reason for that. She knew him better than they did.

Bateman rode up to them and dismounted hastily.

"I heard the shots," he said. "Are you all right?" he asked Liz anxiously.

Something of their feelings for each other must have been in the look they exchanged; Liz could see that Carter was noticing it.

"I'm fine, Sheriff," she said as brusquely as she could, "but they've taken Angie Carter."

"Anyone hurt?"

Liz looked at the dead man, and Bateman's expression hardened.

"All right," he said. "Morris has gone too far." He looked at Carter and said, "I'll get your daughter back for you, Carter."

"I'll get her back myself."

The two men faced each other belligerently and Liz stepped between them.

"Calm down, both of you!" she commanded. "Let's stop and think a moment, and then we'll all get her back."

Morris felt incredible.

Sarah Medford was moaning and crying out beneath him as he drove himself into her. He felt so huge that he would have sworn he was tearing her up inside — and she was loving it!

The feeling of power was unbelievable!

Tracy led the men to the rear of Sarah Medford's house, where he knew that James Morris was once again plowing Sarah's field.

He wondered what the great man would say if he knew that Tracy himself had plowed that same field many times.

"Let her down," he said to Lon, who was riding double with Angie Carter and enjoying it.

Lon handed her down to Tracy, both men using the opportunity to grope her small, hard breasts.

"Get your hands off me!"

"Sure, lady, sure," Tracy said, squeezing her tight from behind. "Be nice now and maybe you and I can have some fun later."

"My father will kill you!"

"He might try."

Tracy turned to Lon and said, "You and the others stay out here awhile to make sure we weren't followed."

"Aw, Jack, we weren't followed, and I was thinking about getting a drink —"

"Do what I tell you!"

Tracy took Angie by the wrist and dragged her toward the house. He intended to barge through the back door, and he hoped he'd be interrupting Morris while he was taking his pleasure.

CHAPTER TWENTY-SEVEN

ANDREW CARTER reached the door of Morris's office a few steps ahead of Bateman and Liz, with Ridge bringing up the rear. They had decided that just the four of them would go to town while the hands stayed to watch the ranch. Carter hit the door with his shoulder and about two hundred pounds of anger and it shattered.

"Morris!" he bellowed.

The others came in behind him and found him standing in the center of the otherwise empty room.

"He's not here," he said helplessly. "And he's not at his house."

They had checked Morris's house, at the north end of town, first. Carter had left the house, too, with a shattered front door.

"Where could they be, then?" he demanded.

"I think I know," Bateman said.

"Where?" Liz asked.

"He's got a woman in a house at the other end of town," the lawman said. "Her name's Sarah Medford."

"How do you know that?" Liz asked curiously.

He smiled and said, "I used to . . . know her."

Liz raised an eyebrow and said, "You think that's where he'll be?"

Bateman nodded.

"All right. Let's take a look."

"Let's go," Carter said, bolting past them toward the door.

Liz grabbed his arm and held him back with great difficulty.

"Let's go easy, Andrew," she said. "If they are there we don't want to force them into anything before we're ready."

Carter was breathing hard, but she could see that he was making an effort to bring himself under control.

"All right," he said finally. "All right. Tell me what to do."

"What do we do with her now?" Tracy demanded.

They were in the living-room of Sarah Medford's house, and he was secretly satisfied that he had indeed pulled James Morris from the grip of Sarah's powerful thighs. He'd been between those thighs himself enough times to know that Morris was feeling a certain amount of anger and disappointment at having to leave that warm and comfortable place.

Morris was wearing his pants and nothing else, and he was clearly uncomfortable.

"As soon as I get dressed," he said irritably, "we'll ride out to the ranch with the paperwork and when Carter signs it he can have his daughter back.''

''You think he'll stand still for that?''

''I think once he has her back he'll be too happy to do otherwise.''

''And the woman? Angel Eyes?''

''Was she there?''

''I didn't see her, but then this little lady practically came walking into our arms.''

''My father won't stand still for this!'' Angie hissed. ''Neither will Liz!''

''I think you're a little too young to make judgements like that, young lady,'' Morris said.

''I'm old enough to know what filth you are!''

Morris took two steps to close the distance between them and rocked Angie's head back with a resounding slap.

Liz suggested they split up and approach the house from different directions. She chose Ridge, which left Carter and Bateman to work as a team.

''Ridge and I will take the front,'' Liz decided.

''I want the front —'' Carter said belligerently, but Liz cut him off.

''You're too emotionally upset, Andrew,'' she said. ''If you break in you're liable to do something that will get Angie killed.''

''She's right, Carter,'' said Bateman.

Carter stared at them for a moment, then turned to Ridge, who stood by expressionless. Liz wondered what the foreman was feeling inside, but at least *he* was maintaining a calm exterior.

''Let me get her out for you, Andrew,'' Liz said. ''Isn't that what you wanted me to do in the first place? Look out for her?''

Carter stood stockstill, his face blank. Then rubbing his hand over his face, he muttered, "All right, all right."

"Shut up!"

"I could shut her up," Tracy said.

He was eyeing Angie speculatively, mentally comparing her with Sarah Medford. Sarah was older and more full-bodied, but there was something about Angie Carter's youth and rangy build — and the memory of how her hard little peach-sized tits had felt in his hands — that made the prospect of bedding her interesting.

"Then you could go back upstairs to —" Tracy started to add.

"Never mind what's upstairs, Tracy," Morris said. "You just make sure no harm comes to this girl until I'm ready to trade her."

"I ain't the one who just bruised her face," Tracy said. Morris looked at Angie and saw the bruise forming on her cheekbone.

"I'm sorry about that," he told her.

"Drop dead!"

His temper flared again, but before he could move to strike her a second time a volley of shots sounded from outside.

Morris looked at Tracy, who said, matter-of-factly, "I guess we won't have to ride out there to make the trade."

CHAPTER TWENTY-EIGHT

CARTER AND BATEMAN approached the back of the house on foot. They soon discovered Lon and the other men milling about behind the house, their horses still lathered from a hard ride.

"They're just sitting around," Carter said, gripping his rifle tightly.

"Your daughter must be inside."

"What are they doing?"

"They're watching," Bateman said.

"For what?"

"For us."

"Well, let's show them —"

"Easy," Bateman said. He put a hand on Carter's arm and could feel how tense the man's muscles were. "We have to wait until Liz and Ridge are in position."

Carter nodded and waited . . . restlessly.

Liz and Ridge moved toward the front of the house and Liz frowned.

"Why don't they have someone in front?"

"They don't expect us to follow," Ridge said. "Morris probably thinks that we'll just sit back and wait for him to contact us about Angie."

"Andrew is going to pieces over this."

"He'll be all right."

"And you?" Liz asked, studying the man's stolid profile. "Will you be all right, Ridge?"

"Yes," the burly foreman answered, and then added, "As soon as we have her back, I will be."

Liz nodded and touched the man's hard, muscled arm in a sympathetic gesture. When this was over the Carters and Ridge would have some talking to do.

"It should be any time now," she said.

He nodded, and they waited.

"Where are we supposed to shoot?" Carter asked Bateman. The rancher flexed his hands, taking first one and then the other off his rifle.

The lawman thought the question over for a moment before answering.

If they fired over the heads of the four, Morris's men would naturally return the fire—and *they* would be shooting to kill. On the other hand, if they picked off one or two of them right away, there'd be less chance of getting shot themselves.

He was lawman, though. By rights he should have called out and given them a chance to give themselves up. Still, he had Angie Carter to think of, and now that Morris had gone this far Bateman doubted he would stop short of killing the girl.

Finally, he made his decision.

"I guess we might as well pick a couple off right away," he said. "How well can you shoot?"

Carter hesitated, then said, "Never had much reason to learn."

"I'll hit what I aim at," Bateman said. "After that all we've got to do is keep the others pinned down until Liz and Ridge can get inside."

"When do we start?"

Bateman drew his gun and said, "Now, I guess."

They both fired.

"Let's go," Liz said, and she and Ridge moved in.

"Get out there!" Morris shouted at Tracy.

"There's enough men out there," Tracy replied, looking toward the rear of the house. "I'd better stay in here."

"Tracy —"

"You better go upstairs and get your gun."

Morris made a grab for his hip and realized that Tracy was right. He was going to need his gun, which he'd left upstairs in the bedroom.

"All right," he said, moving toward the steps. "I'll get my gun."

As he started up the steps Sarah came down, pulling her housecoat tightly closed. "What's going on?" she demanded.

"Get upstairs, Sarah," Morris ordered.

"Jack?" Sarah said, frowning at the other man. She had never expected to see Morris and Tracy in that house at the same time, and she was more than a little stunned.

"Sarah," Morris commanded again. "Upstairs."

Tearing her glance away from Tracy she walked up the steps ahead of Morris.

Suddenly Angie leaped off the couch and ran for the front door.

"Oh, no —" Tracy said, making a grab for her.

At that moment the front door slammed open and Ridge came charging through.

"Ridge!" Angie cried.

"Hold it —" Tracy began, but Ridge slammed into him with the same shoulder he'd used on the door and the man staggered backward and fell.

"Angie —" Ridge said, turning to see if she was all right.

From the floor Tracy rolled over and groped for his gun. He brought it to bear on Ridge, who looked back too late.

"Now —" Tracy said.

Angel Eyes' bullet took Tracy between the eyes and tore the back of his head out. The man sat there as if stunned, and then slowly toppled backward, dead.

"Where's Morris?" Liz asked Angie, who was now within the circle of Ridge's powerful arms.

"Upstairs," she said. "Where's Pa?"

"Out back."

Bateman's first shot took Lon in the chest, knocking him to the ground. The other three men shot back out of reflex, but after a few moments, they decided that a hundred dollars was not enough to die for.

The back door slammed open and Carter and Bateman rushed in. When Carter saw Angie he felt relieved. It didn't dawn on him that she was being held by Ridge in a way that was not purely . . . impersonal.

Or that she seemed to be holding onto Ridge the same way.

"Angie."

"Pa."

Ridge released her and she rushed to her father.

"Baby," he said, hugging her.

"Morris?" Bateman asked after looking at Jack Tracy and satisfying himself that the man was dead.

"Upstairs," Liz replied.

"He's the only one left, then," Bateman said. "I'll go up and get him."

"Why?" Liz asked, holstering her gun. "He's got to come down sometime, doesn't he?"

CHAPTER TWENTY-NINE

BATEMAN LEFT THE HOUSE to get his deputy and the under-taker, leaving Liz and the others to wait out Morris.

"I'll go outside in case he decides to go out a window," Ridge offered.

"Good idea."

"I'll go with you," Angie said. She and Liz exchanged glances, and Liz figured that the girl was about to have her talk with Ridge. After that, it would be her father's turn.

When Liz and Andrew Carter were alone the man seemed to let his guard down a bit.

"God," he said, dropping onto the couch.

"Are you all right?"

"I am . . . now," he said, setting his rifle against the couch. "Now that it's over."

"Angie seems to have stood up pretty well under the pressure."

"That's more than we can say for her father," he said. He removed his hat and wiped the palm of his hand across his sweating brow. "I don't ever want to go through something like that again."

"You won't have to, Andrew," she said. "It's all over."

"Except for Morris."

"He can't go anywhere," she said. "He has to come down sooner or later."

As if on cue, Morris decided to come down sooner.

"Hello, downstairs," his voice called out.

Carter stood up and grabbed his rifle.

"Easy," Liz said. "He's got the woman with him."

"Hey!"

"We hear you, Morris," Liz called back.

"I'm coming down."

"Come ahead, but throw your gun down first."

"Ha!" he laughed harshly. "No way, ma'am. I'm coming down, and I've got the lady with me."

"Damn," Liz swore under her breath.

"He's going to hide behind her," Carter said.

"I don't know what good that will do," Liz said. "He's finished in this town."

"Why not just let him leave?"

"That's not up to us," Liz said. "It's up to Sheriff Bateman."

"I'm coming down!"

"We're ready!"

The stairs creaked as two people started down slowly. After a moment Sarah Medford's legs came into view, clad in riding jeans. Then Morris appeared. He had his left arm around Sarah's waist and was holding his gun in his right hand.

"Back off!" he commanded.

Carter started to take a step back when Liz said, ''We're not going anywhere, Morris, and neither are you.''

Liz noticed then that Morris had a set of saddlebags over his right shoulder. She was willing to bet that they were filled with money.

''I'm leaving, Angel Eyes,'' he said, ''and you aren't about to stop me.''

''Maybe I'm not,'' she said. ''But there's always Sheriff Bateman.''

''Bateman,'' Morris scoffed. ''As long as I've company,'' he said, holding tightly to Sarah Medford, ''I'll go where I please.''

''James, please —'' Sarah said, but Morris squeezed her again, tightly enough to empty her lungs of air.

''Shut up!''

When they reached the foot of the steps Morris said, ''I think I'd like you two to drop your guns.''

''I'm sure you would,'' Liz said, ''but that ain't about to happen.''

Morris eyed her warily, then shrugged as if to say it didn't matter.

''Where's Ridge?''

''Outside, waiting for you to come climbing out a window,'' Liz said.

Morris laughed. ''That's not my style.''

''You don't have a style, Morris,'' Liz said. ''If you did you wouldn't have thrown away everything you had for a little piece of land.''

''I've got enough in these saddle bags to satisfy me and start me off somewhere else.''

''Where the same thing will happen,'' Liz said. ''Your greed will always be your downfall, Morris.''

''You can take the credit for that, lady,'' he said. ''You,

Angel Eyes. I give credit where credit is due. If you hadn't shown up, none of this would have happened. And if Griff Taylor hadn't turned tail and run —"

"You're wrong there, too, Morris."

"What do you mean?"

"Taylor's out there somewhere, waiting for me. Waiting to earn his money."

"He checked out of his hotel."

"You wouldn't understand a man like Griff Taylor, Morris," she said. "A man who will always do the job he promises to do, no matter what it may look like he's doing."

"If that's so then where is he?"

Liz looked toward the door, then back at Morris.

"I'm willing to make a bet with you, Morris," she said. "I'm willing to bet that Taylor knows everything that's gone on over here, and that he's outside now, waiting."

"That's a bet?" he asked. "What're the stakes?"

"No stakes," she said. "A friendly bet. Go ahead. Walk to the door and look outside."

Morris's eyes darted to the door and she could see the curiosity in his eyes.

"I'm going that way anyway," he reminded her.

"Well, go ahead, then."

Liz hoped that Andrew Carter would just sit tight and let her work Morris.

Morris finally began to sidle toward the door, keeping Sarah's body between him and the others. At one point, as he leaned over to look out the window, Liz thought she could have taken him, but she decided not to.

"Sonofabitch," he muttered. He looked back at Liz and said, "The sonofabitch is out there in the middle of the street."

For some reason, Angel Eyes was not surprised.

CHAPTER THIRTY

MORRIS'S NEXT MOVE surprized Liz.

He pushed Sarah toward them, opened the door and rushed out. Carter caught the staggering woman while Liz went out after Morris.

"Taylor, she's here," Morris shouted. "She's in here."

Liz stopped on the porch of the house while Morris rushed out into the street. Taylor was standing there alone, dressed in black, his hooded eyes on Liz.

"You messed up, Morris," he said.

"What?" Morris stopped about five feet away from the man.

"You hired me to do a job, and you didn't have faith in me to do it."

"Do it now, then," Morris said.

"Will you still pay, even though you've lost everything?"

"Yes," Morris said. "Just for my own satisfaction, yes."

He stuck his hand into one of the saddlebags and came out with a fistful of money.

"I'll pay," he said, holding it out to the man.

"Then get out of the street."

Morris looked at Taylor, then at Liz, then stepped aside and off the street.

As Ridge came around the side of the house, followed by Angie, Liz noticed Taylor's companion, John the Beast, for the first time. He was standing off to the side, and as Ridge came into view the two men locked glances. The bigger man moved his eyes, then, from Ridge to Angie, gazing at her hungrily until Ridge deliberately moved between them.

"Taylor," Liz said, "you better call off your pet."

Taylor looked over to where Ridge and John the Beast were facing each other like two warring grizzlies.

"Your friend looks like he can take care of himself," Taylor observed.

Although John the Beast was much taller than Ridge, their muscular development seemed to on a par.

"I promised John that he could have the girl," Taylor said.

"That's crazy," Liz said.

"*You* tell him that."

Ridge spoke up, then.

"I'll tell him."

Taylor's eyebrows went up and he looked interested.

"I'm wondering . . ." he said.

"What?" Liz asked.

"I'm wondering how your friend would fare against John the Beast."

"This is between you and me, Taylor."

"Our business is one thing," Taylor said. "But John wants the girl."

"He'll have to go through Ridge to get her."

Taylor looked at John and called out, "You mind that, John?"

The big man simply shook his head without taking his eyes off Ridge.

"That's it, then," Taylor said.

"Ridge?" Liz called.

The foreman didn't reply.

"Taylor, I hired you —" Morris began to complain, but Taylor cut him off with a glance.

"What's going on?" another voice chimed in, and both Taylor and Liz looked over to find Sheriff Pete Bateman standing with the undertaker, a tall man whose pallor may have been induced by the tense situation.

"Stay out of this, Sheriff," Taylor said.

"I'm the law."

"Pete," Liz said, "this has to be done."

"I can't stand by and watch —"

"Sure you can, Sheriff," Taylor said. "Look at those two," he added, indicating Ridge and John the Beast. "You want to step in between them?"

Bateman looked at the two men and Ridge took his eyes off John just long enough to look at Bateman. The lawman saw the determination in Ridge's eyes . . . and admitted to himself that he was curious.

"Go and clean up," Bateman told the undertaker. "Inside and out back."

The undertaker rushed to do just that, eager and thankful to get out of the line of fire.

"All right, then," Taylor said to Liz. "We back off long enough for your friend and my companion to . . . discuss the situation."

"Fine."

"Liz —" Carter said from behind them.

"Get Angie."

Carter stopped supporting Sarah and went to fetch Angie.

"Pa —"

"Let's go, Angie."

"Ridge —"

"Stay with your father, Angie."

To her father's surprise it was Ridge's command that Angie obeyed. Carter drew Angie over to the front door of the house.

"I'm not going inside," she said.

"What am I thinking of?" he said, and they turned to watch the two muscular men circle each other.

John the Beast moved first, mindful of the erection in his pants. If he couldn't have a woman just yet, why he'd crush this bulky little man in his hands and achieve some sort of satisfaction that way.

Ridge knew his own strength. He also knew that the big man was strong. Ridge's lack of height — due to his short legs — had bothered him as a younger man, but as he grew stronger and more muscular, he learned not to worry about it.

His legs were short, but they were as thick as tree trunks and very powerful. Much of his strength came from those very legs he used to curse.

They'd have to sustain him now as never before.

As the big man approached, Ridge looked into his eyes. They were the eyes of an animal, devoid of intelligence, yet intense. He watched the man's eyes carefully as he started moving forward to meet him.

When the two men clashed Liz swore she could feel the earth move beneath her feet.

Actually, they didn't clash — they crashed!

The two men locked hands; planted their feet and exerted their massive strength. The onlookers' eyes popped as they watched the muscles ripple in the combatants' arms and legs. Try as he might, neither man seemed able to gain the upper hand on strength alone; and yet neither man looked capable of the kind of speed or finesse that might tip the balance between them.

And so they remained that way, locked together. It seemed that stamina alone would ultimately decide the outcome of the battle.

"How long can they stay that way?" Liz heard Angie ask her father.

"I don't know enough about the big man," Carter said, "but I do know Ridge, and I've never known a man with more stamina."

Liz hoped he was right.

Ridge was in trouble.

He wasn't growing weaker, and neither was the other man, but he knew that finally the larger man's legs would make a difference. Being shorter Ridge was forced to keep an upward pressure, while John the Beast was exerting downward pressure. Ridge knew that he would tire first, simply because John was able to *lean* on him.

Still, there was that lack of intelligence in the big man's eyes to work with. John the Beast seemed to operate on instinct alone.

The answer was simple, and if John had been able to think he would have realized it, too.

The pressure being exerted by the taller man was incredible, and Ridge decided that instead of trying to withstand it, he would use it against his opponent.

For one brief moment Taylor thought that John had Ridge, but then he realized what was happening. Ridge's back foot moved — an indication, the gunman first thought, that he was starting to give beneath the pressure. But no; it was that the smaller man had suddenly *stopped* resisting. All at once John was totally off balance, falling toward Ridge.

As the big man staggered forward, Liz saw Ridge close a fist the size of a ham and bring it down on the back of the larger man's neck. She heard John the Beast roar in pain and saw him fight to keep from falling, arms flailing. As he landed he kicked up a huge cloud of dust and Ridge stepped into that cloud, drew back his right foot and kicked the other man in the side. The sound of air escaping from John's lungs was plainly audible. Liz winced as the boot landed.

"That's it," Andrew Carter said, and for a moment he was right. The huge man lay still in the dirt, face down, and it appeared that he was finished.

Then . . .

"Wait," Angie said. "Look."

John was confused, but all he could think of was getting up. He put his hands flat against the ground and pushed himself to his feet. Ridge stepped in to kick again, but this time John caught the foot and yanked, pulling Ridge off balance. This time it was the smaller man who kicked up a cloud of dust.

John was on his feet before Ridge, and closed on the smaller man, wrapping him in his huge arms.

"I guess it's all over now," Griff Taylor called out.

"No it's not," Liz said.

"I've never seen a man break John's bear hug," Taylor said.

"Then watch," Liz said, with more confidence than she felt.

Ridge felt the bones in his back bending; soon they would break. He saw spots before his eyes. His arms were trapped inside his opponent's — as in a bear hug properly applied — and try as he might he could not break the hold. His muscles, rock hard as they were, were useless in this situation.

So he decided to use his head.

He drew his head back and then brought it forward, striking John's forehead with his own. The big man's flesh split and blood poured down over his face.

His reaction was unexpected.

John the Beast had never before experienced pain, and he had never — *never* — seen his own blood, let alone tasted it.

The sensation panicked him, and he released his hold on Ridge and placed his hands over his face, trying to stem the red tide.

He did not see the blow that killed him. Thick as John's neck was, when Ridge swung from his heels and connected with John's jaw, the big man's neck snapped like a twig, and everyone who was watching heard it.

Liz turned to Taylor and said, "Now it's over."

"That leaves us," Taylor said.

"Yes."

Ridge moved in behind Liz and stood next to the Carters. Liz, aware of their presence, stepped off the porch and eased out into the street. With her left hand she reached inside her collar and pulled out the orange bandana that Tate Gilmore had given her. It was her luck; and it was fast becoming her trademark.

The trademark of Angel Eyes.

"Kill her!" Morris shouted at Taylor. "Kill her and I'll pay you plenty!"

Bateman moved in behind Morris and pushed his gun into the man's back.

"You're finished Morris," Bateman said. "As soon as Liz Archer's body hits the ground I'm gonna blow your back out your belly."

"You can't —"

"Just wait and see."

Nervously, Morris watched as Griff Taylor and Angel Eyes squared off, and now he didn't know who to root for. No matter which way it went, he was finished.

And he knew it.

Griff Taylor was working for nothing now, only he didn't know it.

He did know that things had reached the point of no return. Money or no money, it was on!

"There's no edge here for anyone, Taylor," Liz said. "But you sure gave it one hell of a try."

Taylor grinned tightly and said, "I don't need an edge for you, Angel Eyes."

"Fine."

Tate Gilmore's words went through her mind as she watched Taylor's eyes and upper torso. The flick of an eye, he always said, or the twitch of a muscle can be the giveaway. You've got to catch it to capitalize on it.

In Griff Taylor's case he did both, and he died as a result of it.

It happened in slow motion for Griff Taylor, so that he could fully experience every horrifying moment of it.

It was a new experience for the notorious gunman — he was used to being on the giving end of the action — and it was destined to be his last.

Taylor couldn't believe his eyes. His hand flashed for his gun but he hadn't even touched the butt when he saw her gun swing up and extend toward him.

Damn, she was fast!

That was his last thought in life as Angel Eyes pulled the trigger.

Funny, he didn't even feel the bullet hit.

CHAPTER THIRTY-ONE

"DO YOU HAVE TO LEAVE?" Angie asked.

"Yes," Liz said.

She was saddling Blossom at the Paragon Livery. She had already said her goodbyes to both Andrew Carter and Pete Bateman, and in neither case had it been done in bed. To do it that way with each of them — or with one of them rather than the other — just didn't seem right to her.

She had killed Griff Taylor two days before, and already people were coming into town to see where it had happened.

Yes, it was past time for her to leave.

"What are you going to do about Ridge?" she asked Angie.

Angie shrugged and said, "I don't know. I still think he's a little old for me; but maybe we can make it work."

"I'm sure you can, Angie."

"Now all I have to do is convince Pa," Angie said ruefully.

"Liz Archer?" a voice called from behind them.

Both women turned and saw a man standing in the doorway: a tall man wearing a flat-brimmed black hat — and a badge.

Deputy Federal Marshal.

"That's me," Liz said, stepping away from her horse.

The man moved forward and said, "Sheriff said I'd find you here. My name is Earp; Deputy Marshal Earp."

"What can I do for you?"

"I've got James Morris in custody."

"Good. You don't need me to testify, do you?"

"No, but I may need you for something else."

"I don't understand."

Earp reached into a pocket and said, "I've been empowered to offer you this."

When he held the object out to her she saw that it was a badge identical to his.

"A badge," Angie whispered.

"I'm flattered," Liz said, "but I can't accept it."

That didn't seem to bother Marshal Earp. He put the badge away without batting an eye.

"Fine by me," he said. "I can't see a woman as a deputy marshal, anyway."

"Then why offer it?"

"Orders," he said. "Now I can go back and tell the judge I offered and you turned it down." He touched the brim of his hat to them, turned and walked out of the livery.

"That was —"

"I know who it was," Liz said, picking up Blossom's reins.

"But why did you turn him down?"

Liz saddled up and looked down at Angie.

"I've got a reputation whether I want it or not, Angie,"

she explained. "After this thing with Taylor, it'll be a little bigger. I'll have enough people wanting to find me and try me out, not only because of the rep, but because I'm a woman. Wearing a badge would just be like waving a red flag in a bull's eyes."

"I see," Angie said.

"I knew you would."

"Will you come back this way, Liz?"

"I can't say, Angie. Maybe."

Angie smiled and said, "I'm really glad we became friends, Liz."

"So am I, Angie. Good friends are hard to come by, and I count you as one of mine."

Under other circumstances, Liz knew, she and Angie would have been very close friends. Her rep as Angel Eyes, however, had forced her to grow up too fast, adding years to her real age. It would probably continue to do so.

She still had some growing up to do, and she knew that her best chance to stay alive and do it was to keep moving.